PRAISE FOR APPALACHIAN MOUNTAIN MYSTERIES

"The characters come alive because McDaniel takes the time to explore the wellsprings of their pasts and their reactions to adversity. Readers looking for a murder mystery strongly centered in regional culture, the lives and focus of two equally powerful investigators, and a puzzle that draws them into far more than a singular investigation will relish this story's superior tension." **~Midwest Book Review**

"Lynda McDaniel writes wonderful books about human kindness in this series featuring Abit and Della, originally neighbors, but now family. Totally heartwarming and inspirational!!" **~Amazon Customer**

"GREAT !! BOOK Lynda McDaniel can write. This is one fine read. READ THIS ONE." **~Wooley, Amazon Vine Voice Reviewer**

"The most satisfying mystery I've read

in ages." ~**Joan Nienhuis, 1% Top Reviewer Goodreads**

"Five Stars! Lynda McDaniel has that wonderfully appealing way of weaving a story, much in the manner of Fannie Flagg. The tale immediately drew me in, into the town, into the intriguing mystery, and into the people. [This mystery is] a real treat to read and made me anticipate meeting the characters in yet another installment." ~**Deb, Amazon Hall of Fame Top 100 Reviewer**

"Thoroughly enjoyable and intriguing with descriptive powers and beautiful mountain scenery. Intense family and friend dynamics with character vulnerabilities and complex relationships that steal the reader's heart and make this mystery a must-read." ~**Pam Franklin, international bestselling author**

"I was so engrossed in the story that I found it hard to break away for other activities. The author develops the characters in such a way that they feel like friends, and I miss them after finishing the book." ~**D. Tuttle**

FINDING BOOKS YOU LOVE
JUST GOT EASIER

SPELLBOUND MYSTERY MAGAZINE

Spotlight on one author each issue

Insider chat about what we're writing

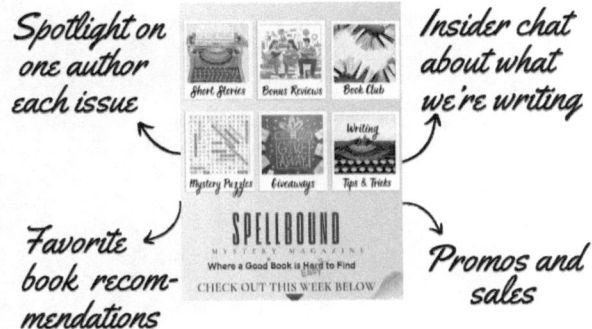

Favorite book recommendations

Promos and sales

MULTIPLE MYSTERY AUTHORS
IN EACH FREE ISSUE

SUBSCRIBE FOR FREE AT
HTTPS://SPELLBOUNDMYSTERYWRITERS.SUBSTACK.COM/

OR SUBSCRIBE BY CLICKING HERE

Deep in the Forest

A Mystery Novel

Lynda McDaniel

Published in 2021 by Lynda McDaniel Books.

ISBN: 978-7346371-4-4

Printed in the United States of America

And into the forest I go, to lose my mind   and find my soul. ~John Muir

Part One

Across the Pond

Prologue: Abit

June 14, 2006

"AM I DEAD?" I whispered in the cold, dark emptiness surrounding me.

Nothing but black strangeness. Not like sleeping. More like being somewhere beyond my ken. When I opened my eyes, not even a crack of light where a window should be.

But if I were dead, surely this wasn't eternity. It was nothing like the glory Mama's church promised if I were good. Not at all like the heaven their unholy hollering cried out about. And I'm shivering from the cold, so it can't be the other place they shouted about even more than heaven (and told me every chance they got *that* was where I was going).

My hand began to feel round, and it landed on a cold, metal frame. I started to laugh—not the kind you do at birthday parties for young'uns or the funny things dogs do. A wicked laugh, me imagining Heaven or Hell like a giant dormitory with all us dead people laid out on long rows of hard, metal beds. Forever.

I shook my head to clear it of such nonsense. It felt like drugs talking. Then a fuzzy memory drifted past, reminding me how late into the evening—yesterday? days ago?—someone gave me a drink and musta slipped something in it. I tried to hold onto that recollection, but it skittered away, outta reach. Then another one followed, of me talking with people I barely knew. And who meant me harm. Some kind of gang Nigel Steadman hooked me up with. I should've known better. Trouble followed that man closer than his shadow.

I still couldn't see anything, but I could smell it. The air in the room hung heavy, dank and musty, like old fruit cellars back home. The ones filled with spiders. I swear I could feel one crawling on me. When I reached to scratch at it, something clanged. My heart beat so hard I could feel its pound *outside* my chest. Then I heard the clang again and knew it was just me, stretching on that good-for-nothing bed.

Gradual-like, my eyes were getting used to the dark. I looked round and could see I was in a finished room, the walls spread out gray and smudged, especially round a shadowy corner cluttered with odds and ends abandoned from long-ago lives.

As I pulled the covers up, I could just make out the sound of someone breathing deeply. I couldn't tell where that was coming from—this room or somewhere nearby? I didn't want to wake it, afraid what that might unleash.

I had no idea how I got there, just that I had been in England, away from my home and my family. My head ached real bad, and I needed to take a leak even worse. But I laid there quiet-like, afraid for my life.

If I still had one.

Chapter 1
Abit

June 5, 2006
Nine days earlier, Atlanta Airport

I PANICKED AS OUR two boys rushed ahead down sprawling corridors, looking for all the world as though they were running away, hurtling toward a future without me. It was ordained they would surely do that someday, *but please not yet* I thought when I could no longer see them. Not till I caught up did my fears ease.

The boys each had their own little suitcase on wheels. Dressed in their Sunday best and pulling the suitcases behind them, they looked like miniature adults, a couple of pint-size salesmen on a business trip. That cracked me up.

I wanted to call out to my wife, Fiona, to look at the boys and enjoy the sight, but she was well ahead of us. There was a fire in that gal, eager to get back to Ireland. Years ago she'd chosen to move to America, but I knew there'd always be a strong pull toward home. *That* home. The magic kind where, thanks to almost four thousand mile and more than a decade, memories hovered lightly, stripped of difficulty or pain. And of course I understood she was eager to be with her family. Who could blame her? It'd been over a year since she hugged her father or sister.

Conor and Vern had gotten ahead of me again, but this time I didn't fret. As I took them in, I felt a powerful pull in my chest. Vern, who'd turned eight year old not long ago, came to live with us after a tragedy that consumed our lives the previous summer. He and our son, Conor, had become like brothers, all but in blood. We were still waiting on the local clerks to do whatever to make it official. They could take forever as far as we were concerned. He was ours, no matter how they saw it, to love and care for every bit as much as our own boy. Truth be known, even Conor had been a gift, of sorts. A mistake that made life perfect.

Those young'uns marched down that long corridor toward somewhere they couldn't yet imagine with a confidence I never had when I was their age. I was too busy getting pulled outta school, feeling like a no count. My daddy, Vester Bradshaw, had given me the nickname that had plagued my early life—Abit, as in "a bit slow." I'd never moved on from that name; it was just what everyone had always called me. Time and self-acceptance had tamed the taint—along with me finally grasping the notion that what Daddy thought of me wasn't gospel. With the help of people who saw something more in me than small-minded parents and town folks of Laurel Falls, I finally found my rightful place in the world. Our farm in the mountains near Laurel Falls and my woodworking turned out to be just right for me. Along with Fiona and the boys and our precious dog, Mollie. And our bluegrass band, the Rollin' Ramblers.

As we walked toward security, I passed a couple holding each other and crying. Next to them, two people were hugging and laughing. I'd seen this at Union Station in Washington, D.C. when I was up visiting my friend Della Kincaid, and now here at the Atlanta airport. It struck me as curious how great happiness and sorrow can stand side by side like that. Sad goodbyes and happy homecomings. And is often the case, give it a few weeks and the tables will turn the other way for those very same folk. I reckon that's not all that different from everyday life. Something bad is always happening, but wait a while and something good eventually comes along.

ONBOARD THE BIG AIRPLANE, the boys got all set up in their seats and given their legs were about a coupla feet long (compared to mine that never seemed to stop), they looked comfortable. They both put their little tables up and down about ten times. Then the flight attendant asked them to keep them upright till we were in the air. Vern had a stack of photos of Mollie he'd brought along with a few clothes pegs so he could put them up wherever he was. He already had two stuck to the little pocket on the seat in front of him.

Conor got kinda upset when a woman across the aisle snuck her tiny dog outta its carrier under the seat. "Why couldn't we bring Mollie like she did?" he whined. I tried to make a joke of it, asking Conor if he could see squeezing fifty-pound Mollie under a seat, her big old fuzzy head sticking out wondering where in the world she was. Conor wouldn't laugh, but Vern chuckled a little. I was about to tell some Mollie stories we all loved when the plane started moving backwards, outta the gate and onto the tarmac.

I'd never been on a plane. Thirty-six year old, and this was a first. I had no idea what to expect. For some stupid reason I'd figured we'd just lift into the heavens, almost like floating. I never expected the raw power that felt both manmade and God-given as we hurtled down the runway, so furious I gripped the armrests and pressed my head against the doily behind my head. I didn't believe in praying to Jesus for little things, like Vern winning his soccer game or the weather turning fine for our family picnic. But this felt bigger than any of that, so I asked Jesus to get us to Dublin safely. I held Conor's hand so tight he whispered, "Daddy," and I eased up. I didn't even know I was doing that. I felt like a fool, but then he squeezed back.

Chapter 2
Abit

June 10, 2006
Five days later, somewhere on the Irish Sea

THE FERRY CHURNED ITS WAY across the Irish Sea, the wind whipping the waters into a frothy stew. A queasiness overcame me so strong I had to head outside for fresh air. When I eased onto the ship's bow, a thick mist wrapped round me like a cold, damp blanket. I braced myself against the railing and watched the fog dance before my eyes, parting from time to time to reveal the shore up ahead, lying in wait.

Everything round me had taken on eerie, wraithlike shapes, only adding to how unreal this trip felt. I'd left my family behind in Dublin to visit England on my own. Hard to believe, given how tucked away I lived in the North Carolina mountains, but here I was now, thousands of miles from home, crossing a sea so roiled I was surprised my breakfast was still with me.

I felt grand.

As I stood there, legs parted and bent for balance, a picture flashed through my mind: the painting of "Washington Crossing the Delaware" hanging in our elementary school back home, something we passed every day so many year ago. Now here I was, standing on the bow, looking across cold, choppy waters just like that great man had oncet done. I laughed at the idea I had anything in common with General Washington.

Looking back, maybe that wasn't as crazy as I'd first thought. Though I didn't know it at the time, I was headed into a long battle of my own.

Chapter 3
Abit

WHEN THE FERRY PULLED in at Liverpool, I couldn't get off fast enough. Not so much because I'd finally made it to Blighty, but the solid footing eased my discomfort from the choppy crossing. Now I needed to find the Lime Street train station and get myself down to a place called Salisbury.

Before I left Dublin, we'd done some sightseeing. Me and the boys loved going to Clifden, where Fiona grew up near the sea. Funny how I'd never been to the Atlantic back in America before I got to see it from the other side, half a world away. When we returned to Dublin, we hung out with Fiona's sister, Elodie, and her father, Quinn O'Donnell. I'd only met him at our wedding almost ten year ago, when he was drunk most of the time. After a health scare the year before, he'd quit drinking—well, for the most part. I'd come up on him taking a nip in the back garden, though I doubted he saw me. Or cared if he had.

Fiona and the boys had made all kinds of plans—she had a big extended family—for while I was away visiting a member of my family, Nigel Steadman. Mine was a found family; folks like Nigel, Alex Covington, and Della Kincaid felt more like kin than any of the Bradshaws.

I was just fifteen year old when Della moved next door to us in Laurel Falls. She'd lived in D.C. her whole life and was some kinda hot shot crime reporter there. But she wanted to get away from all the violence she'd had to write about and bought Coburn's General Store, the store Daddy used to own and let run down to nothing. After a while, though, she started missing some things about D.C.—like museums and cafés and her ex-husband and now-boyfriend, Alex Covington. (Seems they couldn't live with each other—or without.) She'd take the train up for visits, and sometimes I'd tag along.

That's when Della introduced me to Nigel. She'd met him back in the day when he was forging and she was writing. He helped her with background on some mobster story she was working on, and they stayed friends. Eventually, though, "Steady Hand" Steadman got caught and went to work for the Feds, and ... Oh, never mind all that; it's a complicated family history. (Aren't they all?)

Nigel was born and reared in England, but he'd lived in America almost as long. He'd had to flee the U.S. the year before when he got himself mixed up with some no counts in North

Carolina. I'd always had a soft spot for him, even though he was usually getting into some kind of trouble that more than oncet dragged me and Della into it.

We'd talked about how someday I'd look him up in the old country, though I'd only half believed it myself. But here I was doing it. The plan was for me to visit him in London and see the sights, like he'd promised. But when I called from Dublin, I heard one of those weird sounds followed by a message that it was out of service. I dug round in the notebook I carried with me and found a different number to try. The old goat hadn't mentioned anything about moving when he'd given me that number, but that was just like him. And I hadn't thought to ask—I'd just reckoned he'd gotten a new phone. Or a burner, knowing him. It was when I called from Dublin that he told me he'd moved from London to somewhere called the New Forest. I felt my spirits sink. Goodbye London, before I ever met you.

During that call, he stammered and sputtered stuff about how it was too far for me to travel and such. Which was rubbish considering I'd come more than four thousand mile already. Man, that hurt. Coming all that way and not getting to see Nigel—or London—seemed wrong.

"It's not that I don't want to see you, boyo, but it's just that I'm dealing with a spot of bother."

"So what's new ... other than the forest?" I waited for him to say something, so long that I finally had to ask, "Nigel? You still there?"

"Hold on, hold on. Mother of mercy, I'm slipping in me old age. You'll be perfect. See you in Blighty on Monday!" He told me he'd pick me up at the Salisbury station and hung up.

I didn't have a clue what he meant by me being perfect, but I had a feeling it wasn't good.

Chapter 4
Abit

EVEN ONCET I WAS off the ferry, my legs still felt wobbly, and my head spun from all the commotion going on round me. People talking different and hurrying here and there, signs in a bunch of languages, and a general feeling of being somewhere, well, foreign. I made my way to one of the few remaining payphones, looking grand in its little red booth. I had a cellphone Fiona got for me, but in Dublin it didn't work most of the time. Lucky for me Della had given me some pence left over from a long-ago trip to England. She hadn't been able to come back, but she'd held onto the hope—and the coins. I dropped them into the slot. By about the tenth ring, I started to panic. Then I heard a brusque, "Steadman."

"Nigel? It's me, Abit. In Liverpool." Last week when we'd talked, he'd hung up before I felt clear about our arrangements, so I wanted to check in before heading to Salisbury. I didn't trust him not to have moved again!

"Ah, hello, hello, hello, Abit. You called just in the nick."

My stomach knotted. "What does *that* mean?"

"Not to worry, Abit. Just a figure of speech."

"I've been studying the map and train schedules. According to this brochure, I should be in Salisbury by two o'clock."

"I'll pick you up in front of the station. I'll be driving a black taxi. And don't forget to look both ways before crossing. I'd hate for you to come all this way only to get flattened by a left-driving lorry."

I'd already been pulled back to the curb a time or two in Ireland, so I knew what he was talking about. But then something hit me. "Hey, Nigel, I thought you didn't drive."

"Oh, again, just a figure of speech. We'll see you soon, boyo. Bye-ee." He hung up before I could ask anything more.

The train from Liverpool to Salisbury pulled in right on time, and I hopped aboard. I loved trains. The Southern Crescent from Charlotte up to D.C. carries some of my best memories from when I was a teenager, but I found the British Railway cars even nicer. I especially liked the tea lady selling, among other things, scones and tea. I ordered two of each. She looked round for the second person, then gave me a funny look. Probably thought I was a greedy American, but I was well over my seasickness. I slathered on butter and raspberry jam and gobbled them down, as by then we were fast approaching Salisbury.

I made my way to the front of the station where a lashing rain greeted me. The wind blew cold down my neck and gave me a shiver. In June! By now back home guys were wearing short-sleeved shirts and girls were slipping round in those fine sundresses they favored this time of year. Fortunately I'd packed a light coat.

I looked up just as Nigel stuck his head out the window of a black taxicab and shouted: "Hop in, Abit—and look both ways!"

When I'd visited Della in D.C., I always felt like a king riding in a cab. I even got brave enough to hail them. I'd never had something so powerful do my bidding, with just a flick of the hand. But this one was even better, looking like one of those old cars in 1940s movies. Big, boxy, and black from head to toe, including the leather upholstery.

It'd been close to a year since I'd seen Nigel, but we had a typical English reunion: solid handshakes and a brief nod to mark our reunion. I wanted to throw my arms round him, but I knew better. (Little did I know by the end of my visit, I'd want to clutch my hands round his neck. Tight.)

I tossed my grip in the backseat and hopped in the front. Nigel pulled round other cars waiting for passengers and took off. While he drove, I studied him some. He looked good. Last time I'd seen him he'd let himself go: mussed hair, stubbly face, flannel shirt and jeans from the dry goods store in town. He'd returned to his sartorial splendor, as Della called it, in a custom-tailored suit and that Fred Astaire look with his silvery hair. And of course he was wearing a silk tie, something I hadn't worn since Mama's funeral a few year ago.

As he drove, we talked some about our lives and our families. But mostly I lost myself in the beauty of Salisbury as we passed the cathedral and crossed the River Avon. Even I'd heard of that river. (Nigel later told me that wasn't Shakespeare's Avon but one of nine River Avons. Kinda confusing, if you asked me. Seemed Avon is Welsh for river, but even so, I couldn't figure why anyone would want to name a river River River.) As we headed farther into the country, Nigel barreling along narrow roads, my heart stopped. "Wait a minute, Nigel. This is way more than a figure of speech. You told me and Della you never learned to drive."

"Well, not officially, I suppose, but what's so hard about keeping the wheel steady and your foot on the accelerator?" He laughed, threw the car into fourth, and plowed ahead. He glanced over, and I knew without the help of a mirror what my face looked like. "Not far now, laddie boy. Not far now," he sang out, as though that would calm my nerves.

What did take my mind offa his driving was the countryside, which had turned all crazy quilt, patches of green divided by hedgerows and dry stone walls, a lot nicer than miles and miles of the barbed wire fencing we had back home.

The weather rode along like a third passenger. At times it was a moody traveler, demanding our attention with heavy bouts of rain, only to become sunny, leaving everything scrubbed clean till it almost sparkled.

Nigel finally pulled into the parking area at an old hotel, the Bridgewater Arms, and I let out my breath. (I hadn't realized I'd been holding it.) What a fine building—stucco walls up to its thatched roof, surrounded all round with baskets of flowers. I wondered if other people on their first trip to England felt like they'd waked up in a fairytale.

I figured we were just stopping for a beer and a bite to eat, but Nigel grabbed my grip and headed through the front door. What a sight inside. Panel after panel of warm wood and upholstered furniture and a crackling fire taking the chill off the day. Nigel walked to the reception desk and spoke in a low tone to the clerk, then turned to me. "We're putting you up here, Abit. The owner's an old friend of mine. Owes me a favor. Gave me a big discount, and the club will pick up the rest. I just don't have enough room at my place."

I was relieved to hear that, given I hadn't counted on paying for a room this fancy, if at all. But I knew it came at a price. I hated to think what it would cost me in other ways. I didn't want to ask him about that in front of the staff, so I just said a genuine thanks. I was too weary then to think about consequences, though I did wonder what the *club* was.

While they fixed up my room, we stopped off at the beer garden. Right away I noticed that dogs were welcome—not the way they do back home where they act like dogs carried the plague. I thought of Mollie as I patted the fur of a sleepy retriever below the table next to ours.

"Let's have a pint, Abit. Just like we did back in D.C. at the Churchill Arms. Different arms, different country, but we can toast your being this side of the pond."

"My treat, for picking me up and all," I said. He waved me off and went to the bar. When he came back, he was carrying two brimming pints—one looked too pale to be beer, but he placed the amber-colored one in front of me. A waiter soon followed with the menu. I ordered chicken and mushroom pie with gravy, vegetables, and little potatoes. Nigel said he'd already eaten.

"Here's to a good visit, Abit." We clinked glasses. "My friends are all anxious to meet you."

"Why would they be anxious to meet me?"

"Oh, now, don't start that self-effacing crap again. I thought you were over all that."

"And I thought you were over all *your* crap."

He laughed, then tried for a face that said he didn't know what I was talking about. "Whatever do you mean?"

Maybe I was being rough on him. Maybe not. "Oh, nothing, Nigel. Just sounds like you might have something up your sleeve."

He choked a little on his drink and turned serious-like. "Well, actually, Abit me boy, I do."

Chapter 5
Abit

AFTER LUNCH, WE CHATTED a while before Nigel headed home to "gather information for our meeting with the club." There it was again. The club. And he wouldn't tell me more. I decided to stop worrying and take a walk in the New Forest. It may not be London, but I was almost as keen to see what the woods were like over here. The woman at the hotel front desk gave me a brochure and map for a "cheery stroll into a nearby wooded glade."

I learned that even though it's called a forest, that doesn't mean just trees. Forest was a legal term that referred to an area where the upper crust could hunt without being bothered by riffraff like me and my kind.

I felt all sorts of tensions lift as birdsong surrounded me; even the mournful cry of a hawk sounded welcoming. The trees were shot through with every shade of green imaginable, and even the air had a special scent. I passed a lovely little pond and what the brochure called a shack. (That musta been the British definition because it looked a lot nicer than any of ours back home.) The dappled sun on the leaves in the trees and those blanketing the ground made me happy. I wasn't sure if it was Fiona's influence on me or my heritage grabbing hold, but I couldn't recall ever feeling so at home.

As the path wended its way in a loop, I passed grazing sheep and walked through an archway of yellow-blooming laburnum. My favorite tree. Funny how I was eager to go somewhere new but felt both comforted and excited by something familiar. Then again, the sight of one (let alone twelve) blooming laburnums is enough to make anyone's heart beat fast.

Back at the inn, I needed a rest before the meeting that evening, whatever that held in store. I lay on my bed, hands behind my head, looking round the room. It was every bit as nice as the rest of the place. I admired the craftsmanship of the old furniture and the tea table where they'd supplied me with my own electric kettle, tea bags, ceramic cups, and even milk and sugar, right there like room service whenever you wanted. The only time I'd had room service was almost twenty year ago, back when Della and I stayed in a fancy hotel in Atherton, Virginia. We were on the trail of those con artists who'd screwed me and my school, the Hickson School of American Studies, outta lots of money and good intentions. I'd never forgotten the feeling room service gave me of being cared for without having to lift a finger, and this seemed just as good.

Before I nodded off, I thought about how lucky I was. Later, I'd come to regret this lapse in my usual caution. Seriously, no wonder people were superstitious.

I WOKE GROGGY FROM a deep sleep, the kind where you have to peel yourself offa the sheets. I made another cuppa in my room, freshened up a bit, and headed down to the pub. I could get used to living this way.

While I waited for Nigel, I overheard two grown men come to fisticuffs over soccer, or rather football, as they call it. Nigel walked up just before the publican had to throw them out. I said something about it being too nice a place for the likes of that, but Nigel just shrugged. "Football means the world to a lot of blokes. Some of them don't have much else in their lives."

Folks back home were the same. I wished everyone coulda gone to The Hicks, where we were taught how creative we naturally are. Funny that I had to get thrown outta regular school to find that one, but I was grateful how things had turned out. Making furniture and music meant the world to me. If I hadn't come on them the way I did, I'd probably be drinking and fighting over something as stupid as a leather ball.

I'd gotten my money exchanged at the front desk and bought Nigel and myself each a pint. It felt grand to walk up to the publican to ask for a Guinness and Old Speckled Hen. Nigel clinked my dimpled beer mug but didn't take a sip from his. He was awful quiet, just looking round for his friends to arrive. When they finally showed up, they were a strange looking group if I ever saw one. (And believe me, I'd seen loads of strange over the years.) In that gentlemanly fashion he had, Nigel made introductions: Marcia, Graham, and Malcolm. We shook hands.

We gathered in one of the inn's backrooms, round a big wooden table next to a glowing fireplace. The evening had returned to damp and chilly. Well, actually cold, so I was grateful for the fire. That room, too, had the same fine wood paneling as mine upstairs. The ceiling came down low with dark beams, and framed hunt scenes filled the walls. A dartboard hung against the far wall.

Finally, Nigel cleared his throat. "You're probably wondering why we called this meeting."

"Well, no probably about it," I said, the pint making me more direct than usual. Everyone turned to look at me. "I came to visit my old friend Nigel, but I have a feeling it's not as simple as that." Everyone chuckled, though I hadn't meant to be funny. My stomach knotted. I watched as they all sized me up like a 4H heifer at the county fair, and not the one likely to win the blue ribbon. "Okay, Nigel, what's going on?"

"Well, you see, laddie boy ..."

He hemmed and hawed until I said, "Don't go mixing me up in your troubles."

They all nodded at each other with big smiles. Someone murmured, "Oh, yes. That will do nicely."

"What would do nicely?"

"We need you," Nigel said.

I got a real bad feeling. "Well, I don't hold with that," I said as I pushed my chair back from the table, stood, and headed to my room as though I knew what I was gonna do next.

"Now, listen, Abit. This won't bring any trouble to your doorstep, I promise."

Nigel was sitting on the chair across from my bed, where I lay on my back, staring at the ceiling. He'd come up to my room to try to talk me into doing his bidding, something I knew all too well would come to no good.

"Oh, yeah? Like that Johnny Ray Meeks character you brought to my farm, the one who scared my boy so bad?" I felt all wound up, waving my arms round. "I know what you bring to a doorstep, whether it's back home or the New Forest."

"It's nothing like that, I promise. There's no scheme or forgery involved. Just a little detective work—like you and Della are so good at."

Well, he had me there. Della and I had done enough capers that it would be hard to act like I didn't know what he was talking about. "But I'm on vacation, Nigel. You know, a little drinking, walking in the New Forest, seeing the sights."

"Exactly. That's all we want from you. You'll meet some new people at another pub, and you can still go on walks and such. Marcia even volunteered to take you to Stonehenge."

"Well, la-di-dah. You make it sound like she's making a big sacrifice." I paused and thought about what'd I just said. "Okay, maybe she is, but you and I were supposed to do stuff together. And I don't appreciate your springing this on me with all those ne'er-do-wells looking on."

"Now just one minute, Abit. Those are my friends, and I don't believe you know anything about their do-wells."

"My point exactly."

"One is a retired doctor, another a computer expert, and Marcia is a very good lip reader."

"If they're so fine and upstanding, why don't they do their own investigating?"

"Because all the people involved in this, er, spot of bother know them. None of them know you. And that Southern accent of yours will charm them, keep them from thinking about any ulterior motives."

"And just what are the ulterior motives?"

Nigel sighed. "Okay, I get it. You deserve a better explanation. I was wrong to keep you in the dark so long. I was afraid you'd say no. I was too clever by half."

"You can say that again."

"I was too clever by half."

Corny, but still it made me laugh. Then we got down to business.

Chapter 6
Della

ABIT AND THE KIDS had been gone only a few days, but knowing they were out of arm's reach made me miss them all the more.

I was driving over to their farm in the small community of Hanging Dog to check on things, especially Mollie. Somehow my dog, Rascal, a little feist who'd taken up with me the year before, knew where we were headed and began whining and carrying on in the front seat just a few minutes after pulling out of Coburn's parking lot.

As we made our way up their drive, Mollie came bounding out from behind the farmhouse. I barely had my door open before Rascal jumped out and began rolling around on the grass with her. I was all but forgotten. Until I picked up Mollie's food bowl; she gave Rascal a quick look before running over and trilling at me as I filled her bowl with kibble.

It seemed every summer got hotter and dryer than the last, and this one was no exception. But out here on the farm, surrounded by tall pines and mountain vistas, it felt cooler. I walked around the yard and over to the garden, a good place for sorting out my thoughts.

Something was wrong at my store, Coburn's General Store, and I needed help unraveling the mess the books were in. I was dreading my trip to Asheville later that afternoon to meet with a forensic accountant. I'd checked and double-checked invoices, comparing stock to sales for months. They just didn't jibe. With a little detective work on my own, I'd determined the problem had started well before my new assistant, Annie Totherow, came to work in March. Bookkeeping wasn't my favorite part of storekeeping, but I was pretty good at it. Or I *thought* I was. Whatever, I needed professional answers.

I went back to where Mollie and Rascal were playing and gave them some special treats I'd brought from the store. I threw a stick for them to fetch, though they grasped the stick a lot better than the concept of letting it go. I gave up after a while and sat on the porch swing. I could feel the adrenaline easing out of my body as I enjoyed its peaceful rhythm.

I was being soothed by a mockingbird's song when I heard, "I see you've come to do your duty." That would be Shiloh. He had a way of ruining a Zen moment, even though he claimed to be a Zen master. He was a great craftsman and a big help to Abit with his woodworking business, but his personal skills weren't as finely tuned as his dovetail joints. He walked up the porch steps and surprised me when he sat down on the swing. (I was glad to note his patchouli phase had finally passed.) "Yeah, it's nice out here," he said. "You seem a little tense."

I had to give the guy credit. He had a sixth sense about situations. Or was I that obvious? "Just the usual workaday stuff," I said.

"You need to meditate more."

"So I can be more like you?"

"Well," he said, a little prickly, "you could do worse."

I laughed. He was right—on all counts. He smiled, and we sat quietly together until the dogs came looking for more water, both of them wet from grass and slobber. I combed Mollie's luxurious wiry fur; I didn't want Abit to come home to a matted mess. Then I put out more treats for her and said goodbye to Shiloh. Rascal and I headed to Asheville.

IT WAS LATE IN the day when we arrived at the Grove Park Inn. In spite of the financial troubles at Coburn's, I couldn't resist staying at the grand old hotel. Its Arts and Crafts style always awakened my own creativity, in keeping with the mission of that movement. The beauty of the materials used—enormous granite boulders and massive wood beams—brought nature indoors, mirroring its elegant simplicity.

I didn't even need to sneak Rascal in. He was considered a "registered resort pet guest." Whatever, it sure beat stuffing him into a carryall to hide him (something I'd done a time or two at other hotels). On a lark, I'd tried making a reservation for either Room 441 or 442, but they were always booked ages in advance. That's where F. Scott Fitzgerald stayed in 1935 and '36 while Zelda spent time in a nearby asylum. Fitzgerald's typewriter was on display somewhere in the inn, and that plus the spirit of Thomas Wolfe hovering around the town made it a dream destination for writers. It had been more than twenty years since I could claim that honor—I just seemed to write checks these days—but I still felt it in my bones.

We found our more ordinary room in the Vanderbilt wing, though it was plenty luxurious with its fluffy white robes and all those little bottles of creams and lotions that smelled exquisite. Quite a change from our scaled-down life in Laurel Falls. But to be fair, my home above Coburn's was everything I'd ever hoped for.

I fed Rascal and made sure he was a comfortable resort pet guest before heading down to the Sunset Terrace, the outdoor restaurant overlooking the mountains. I spent a little time walking around the hotel, running my hands along the beautifully crafted furniture. I'd read the Arts and Crafts furnishings alone were worth $4 million. I stopped in the lobby, where ten U.S. Presidents had visited, and admired the cavernous stone fireplace. And of course I looked for the Pink Lady, the ghost of a guest dressed in a pink flowing gown who reportedly fell to her death in the inn's Palm Court in the 1920s. Apparently she never checked out.

As you might expect, the prices at the restaurant were astronomical, so I opted for the cheapest entrée: Roasted Airline Chicken / herb dumplings / roasted carrots / local greens / roasted chicken jus. Not sure why anyone would even hint at airline food in the menu copy, but I supposed there was some reason for that adjective. Looking back, maybe it was a sign—that I'd soon be on a long flight needing sustenance, though that didn't even register as a vague notion at the time.

As I ate, the sunset behind the mountains made the pricey meal worth every penny—what the guidebooks call "sweeping views and stunning sunsets." Vibrant reds and purples chased off the more demure pinks as the sun slowly slipped away. I sipped my glass of viognier, and the relaxed atmosphere gave me a chance to digest what the accountant had told me. We had more work to do, but she saw enough signs that someone had been stealing from the store to suggest I gather more ledgers and files and come back in a week.

Strange thing was, the thefts were never in cash, just food. Maybe that didn't seem as larcenous to the perpetrator. I knew people went hungry in our community, and they'd be welcome to some extra food if they'd asked (though I knew that was hard for them to do). I had a barrel off to the side where I put things close to expiration—still good and free for the taking. Trouble was, most of the takers could well afford them. Maybe I'd start taking the items to a food bank instead of offering them to the un-needy.

Whoever was responsible had been at it for almost a year. They must have been good because I never suspected a thing. Then again, I'd been lulled into a sense of security with my regular customers. Over the years, though, with the influx of second-homers, I no longer knew everyone who shopped at Coburn's.

Or maybe someone held something against me. I didn't think the Holt family—Astrid, Dee, and Enoch—would bother. Besides, Abit and I had *helped* them find out what happened to their family, even though we never really told them what happened. I thought about Blanche Scoggins, who owned the laundromat and hated me on general principle. Actually, she hated the entire population of Laurel Falls, but especially me and Abit for what took place almost twenty years ago. Long time to hold a grudge, but then mountain people would crush the competition if grudge-carrying ever became an Olympic sport.

Chapter 7
Abit

"WHERE DID YOU LEARN to talk like that?" Marcia was the first to ask me questions.

"Well," I replied, "I reckon I could ask the same of you." She smiled and nodded approval—of what, I still wasn't clear.

Nigel had called another meeting with his gang, though earlier they'd looked offended when I'd called them that. They told me they thought of themselves as truth seekers, which sounded like some of Shiloh's mumbo-jumbo. And they were a *club*, they said, not a gang.

"Can you lay that accent on a little thicker?" Graham asked.

"What accent?" I replied. Smiles all round. As if they didn't sound funny when they traveled somewhere else in the world.

The night before, Nigel'd convinced me to meet again the next morning to learn more about his so-called spot of bother. The *club* had all returned to the pub, hanging out in the bar till we sat down for lunch. Marcia nodded toward a scruffy looking guy standing nearby.

"Nigel said you wanted to meet some of the local folk. Go have a chat with Thomas. He'd be a good one to practice on."

"What do you mean by *practice*?" I asked. She just shooed me over to a rather hapless fellow.

His face, rutted like a fallow field left to crack in the summer sun, was framed by long greasy hair. But when he smiled, only his gold front tooth shined brighter. Thomas asked me a bunch of questions about America (some I couldn't answer), and oncet he found out I lived on a farm, he launched into tales about growing up on a dairy farm. "A lot of milkin' and muckin', but it was worth it to gaze into their gentle brown eyes of a morning."

I coulda listened to him all day, but Nigel called me to lunch. I excused myself. "We'll have to talk more about *you* next time," Thomas said with a wink that somehow made its way out from the deep crevices round his eyes.

Nigel pulled me toward a backroom in the inn. (I'd've rather talked with Thomas than the club, but that would have to be another time.) When we sat down, Marcia murmured something about Thomas being a right old anorak, and everyone laughed.

"What's an anorak?" I asked.

"A jacket," Nigel answered.

"Why would you call Thomas a jacket?"

Oh, they thought I was hilarious, but their laughter at my expense was getting old. Nigel read my face. "Now don't pay them any mind,

Abit. But really your visit couldn't come at a better time."

"Quit saying that and explain yourself."

"That's what we're about to do."

I'D FINISHED MY PLOUGHMAN'S lunch, which came with all kinds of things I love—crusty bread, cheeses, salad, pickled onions, Branston pickle. Fiona made them at home, but this one tasted even better, the sharp, crumbly English cheddar unlike anything we could get in Laurel Falls. Nigel ordered a steak and kidney pie with a perfectly browned crust and a hole in the middle for the steam—and aroma—to waft out. The others just ordered more beer and crisps (aka *potato chips*).

I must have passed some kind of test talking with Thomas, because all the jokiness went out of their explanations about what lay ahead. Bear with me here—it had all the twists and turns of a Nigel caper, only this time he seemed in the right.

Someone had stolen a bunch of fence-able stuff from a big manor house, and the police arrested Nigel's girlfriend, Nigella. (I looked over at him, my expression asking, "*Really? Your girlfriend is named Nigella?*" but he refused to look my way.) He explained for my benefit that she had form, or what we call a rap sheet, and a detective found three or four stolen items stashed in her greenhouse behind her house. "She told me she hadn't grown so much as a radish in there for years," Nigel added. "She had no idea what was back there."

But there was more. Nigella was known for her safecracking skills. Nigel got darned near misty eyed when he described her "delicate little hands." At the manor house, someone had opened the safe in an upstairs bedroom—the owners swore they hadn't touched the safe in weeks—but all prints had been wiped clean. They kept mostly jewelry in there, which had all been taken along with some cash. Unfortunately for Nigella (assuming I believed she was innocent), someone had tossed a brooch in her front garden—and she'd fenced it. "Like an idiot," Nigel added, likely a comment he would have kept to himself if his delicate-handed girlfriend had been there. "She should have smelled a setup, but she told me she needed the money."

"So does she have an alibi?" I asked.

"She couldn't have done it." Nigel insisted.

"But what do the police say?" I noticed I was the only person asking questions. The others were looking all round or fiddling with their pint glasses.

"That she doesn't have an alibi," Nigel said rather indignantly. I kept waiting for a better answer than that, and he finally snapped at me, "She was with me that night! Okay?"

At first I didn't think anything of that. It wasn't until a minute later the penny dropped. No wonder everyone had gone so quiet—Nigel had conveniently forgotten to tell me how the rest of the story played out. I stared at him until he added, "Okay, I will testify that she was with me, but only if I have to."

"Go on," Graham said. "Explain to the boy."

I hated how people always called me boy. I was thirty-six year old, for crying out loud. Vern and Conor were *boys*. But I just nodded. No need in distracting Nigel from getting on with it.

"Her husband, Miles, is a good friend of mine. Of all of us," he finally said, motioning round the table.

Some friend you were to him, I thought. I wasn't such a *boy* that I didn't know these things happened, for all kinds of reasons, but still, this sounded like a strange friendship to me. "Don't tell me," I said, my words laced with sarcasm, "he's away in prison, and she got lonely."

"No, no, nothing like that. He's actually an accountant and went down to London for work." I didn't want to think about why Nigel was best friends with an accountant. He went on. "Thing is, the bottle and stoppers (aka *coppers*) will just say she was the mastermind. Didn't have to be there."

"But what about the safecracking?" I asked.

"Well, there is that. Okay, okay. Like I said, I will come clean if I have to. But that's why we need your help. We're trying to return things to normal without any true confessions. Besides, you owe me."

Oh, I knew he'd drag that out before we'd finished. I wondered when this debt would ever be repaid—the fact that Nigel got me and Fiona back together after we went through a rough patch. Was there no end to it? Still, I thought of Conor coming along not long after that and nodded for him to go on.

I listened with one ear and studied the odd collection that made up this so-called club. I'd never been in a foreign country before, and I couldn't help but ponder how we were different and yet the same.

Marcia made me think of Della. She had a pretty face and lovely voice, and she seemed kind, yet lively and spirited at the same time. She had a long mane of dark hair that had kept its shine and sported only a few streaks of gray. Graham was kinda stuff-shirty, making me think of Sheriff Horne. The kind of person who seemed like his chest was always thrust out, even though it was really tucked inside his shirt normal-like.

I didn't want to keep comparing them to people I already knew—why bother to travel if that's all you did? I wanted to meet characters I hadn't seen before, like Thomas. I got my wish when a man dressed in a navy suit coat over a yellow sweater vest and colorful striped tie walked in—wearing a boater with the top cut out of it.

At this point, Nigel realized I hadn't had a chance to talk to anyone other than Graham. (I'd sat next to him at lunch, but we'd only chit-chatted.) For the most part, all I knew were their first names. I didn't even know the new fellow's name, though I soon learned it was Roy Arthur Lewis.

"Let's all go round and tell the lad about ourselves," Nigel said. "Some of you could go on for hours, but try to keep it short." Not everyone chuckled at that. I figured the straight faces belonged to the longwinded ones.

Roy Arthur pulled out a pack of Gauloise and stunk up the place. I was used to tobacco smoke. When I was growing up, farmers relied on—even prized—their burley tobacco allotment. It seemed everyone used tobacco, be it smoked, chewed, and/or spat. Lately, all that had changed with new government programs, but people still smoked like chimneys. While he puffed on his fag (that's what Marcia called it when she asked if he *had* to smoke that thing inside), Graham jumped in, seeming like the kind of guy who doesn't like to mess about.

"Abit, you and I talked some over lunch, but we didn't get past the small talk. I'm the club's computer and internet nerd. I can find just about anything you need to know, and I can hack my way into networks better than your CIA."

"Don't hold back, Graham," Nigel said. "No need for modesty among friends." Everyone laughed at that. He *was* kinda full of himself.

Next came Marcia, who was waving her hand in front of her face, as if that did any good getting rid of the smoke in such a small room. "Well, dear, I am a former farmer—and I understand you are still one, so jolly good for us! But my claim to fame with the club is that I'm a crackerjack lip reader. My parents were both deaf, and I know sign language as good as Charles Michel de l'Eppe himself. And alongside that comes lipreading and lots of patience." She nodded her head to indicate she was finished.

"How do you use lipreading for the club?" I asked.

"Oh, you'd be amazed. And truth be told, what I do is more like what's called speechreading—lips, tongue, cheeks, eyes, expressions, gestures—so I can gather enough clues to understand not only the words but the intentions of the speaker. I can stand in a pub, for example, or across a public square and glean information from just about any conversation." She took off her glasses and cleaned them on her blouse (a black silk one that wouldn't show the dirt), and sounded a little sad when she added, "though my eyes aren't what they used to be."

The club was politely quiet for a moment before Malcolm spoke up. "Well, I'm a doctor, but I hang out with this crazy club because I'm long-retired and get bloody bored at the house with the missus. Don't get me wrong. She's a finer woman than I deserve, but still, I need an interest outside the home."

I figured there was more to that story than he was telling. "Do you need to do a lot of bandaging for the club?" I heard my voice come out kinda high, which of course made them laugh.

Malcolm smiled kindly at me. "No, Abit, I don't. Just the odd scrape from time to time."

"Yeah, remember that time Nigel had to escape out the back and got tangled in the brambles?" That was Roy Arthur Lewis.

"Oh, Roy, put a lid on it! Time is short. Let's move on," Nigel interrupted.

Roy tipped his topless hat and said, "Don't have a lid to put on it."

Again, everyone laughed, even Nigel. I had to hand it to them; they were a jolly club of misfits. Nigel looked over my way. "We tend to get easily sidetracked, Abit. We've known each other for donkey's years. We know which party each other votes for, what our personal lives entail, and so on. So Roy, why don't you tell Abit about your musical skills?"

"Before we get to that, Nigel, I'd like to add something for Abit," Marcia said. "He needs to understand that we consider ourselves fam." When I looked puzzled, she added, "That's slang for friends, really good friends." Everyone nodded, including me. I could see they were close, and the club felt real to me for the first time.

"Thank you, Marcia, for that clarification," Nigel said, sounding a bit pompous. "Now Roy?"

He spoke in a quiet, halting way, explaining his love of music. That perked up my ears, and of course I felt an immediate connection to him. I asked what instruments he played, and he blushed. Graham chimed in, "Fiddle, guitar, bass, mandolin, cello, and piano. At last count!" Roy Arthur lit another Gauloise and shifted the subject to his work as a music teacher.

When he was through talking, I still had a question. "But what do you do for the club?"

"He's an old friend, but mostly we brought him in special for you," Nigel said. "We've used him a time or two before. Amazing how music takes people's minds off of what's right under their noses."

Part of me hated to think about music being used in some kinda underhanded way, but I knew what Nigel was talking about. Whenever I play, it takes me to another—and better—place.

Two latecomers eased in and sat at the other end of the table, away from Nigel holding court up front. One looked like a professor, his gray curly hair going off in tangents. He bummed a cigarette from Roy Arthur Lewis and busied himself with all that involved. Nigel spoke for him. "Alfred here had a distinguished career in the British Army, serving his country in

Afghanistan. Since then, he has chosen to lead a quieter life." Nigel gave me a look that said *don't ask any questions!* Then he introduced Roger Dalton.

Dalton stood up and kinda bowed. Then he cleared his throat and shot his cuffs. Man, he was more dolled up than Nigel: tie, tie pin, crisp white shirt with fancy cuffs set off by gold cufflinks, light-blue waistcoat, black suit coat, and trousers with a perfect crease. Come to find out he was a former rock and roll star. I'd never heard of him, but that didn't mean anything. He caught me studying his spotless attire. "I wasted all those youthful years wearing smelly jeans and dirty shirts. I'm making up for it now." His smile stretched clear cross his face.

I thought about how the money for his outfit coulda kept my boys clothed for a year, and as though he could read my mind, he answered my unasked question. "I made good money as a musician, and I've made even better investments. You might say I'm the bankroller for the club. If you need anything as you do your work, just let Nigel know, and we'll get it for you."

I hadn't agreed to do any "work" yet, and I didn't like the idea of needing money or equipment in the process. But I thanked him all the same. I had one more question before I hoped this long meeting would finally end. "And what about Nigella?" I asked.

"What about her?" Nigel asked.

"Where is she?"

"In jail, you berk! That's why we need a plan to get her out."

Well! That didn't sound like the Nigel I knew, and I didn't like his tone one bit. I got it that he was upset about Nigella, but he was out of order. I could feel my face flush. "So you're just staying quiet while she's stuck in the slammer?"

"That's it, boyo—either her marriage goes broke or she spends a bit of time in the nick. She doesn't love me, and she told me she'd rather sit in jail than lose Miles. So it's her choice, not mine."

I shook my head at his logic, though in a strange way I guessed it made sense. I took a sip of my beer and calmed down. This had all been a bit too much.

Graham cleared his throat and tapped his dinner knife on his pint glass. "I've got something to report." Everyone quieted down, looking eager for his news. "I tried searching a few likely persons who might have committed the theft. No one I found could have done it for a variety of reasons. But as I went deeper, I discovered someone you may have heard of but I hadn't: Clive Ownbey. He's the kingpin of a gang once headquartered in Bournemouth, though they've now moved north into Hampshire. I'll keep checking my sources to learn more, but I did find out they hang out at the Dog & Bone just beyond Ringwood."

They all began murmuring. It was clear most of the club knew this guy—except for Graham, who probably didn't get out that much, what with his computer work and all. It was also clear they didn't like Ownbey.

"Let's case the Dog & Bone," Malcolm said.

That got them going until Nigel interrupted. "Don't forget there's bloody CCTV everywhere, so we need to be careful. And we don't know whether or not some coppers are in cahoots with Ownbey." He paused, like he was uncertain about what he wanted to say next. "That's where you come in, Abit. They don't know you—and they don't know you know us—so you can't be seen with any of us. So no more cavorting at the bar here—we'll meet always in a closed room and leave separately. When we go to the Dog & Bone, we hope they'll surmise that is the only place you've come into contact with us. Just by chance. And not a dicky bird (aka *word*) about us when you talk to them."

Everyone looked at me, so I nodded just to be polite. And wouldn't you know it? They took that as a yes, that I was in. If I'd known the trouble that nod would cause me, I'd've said *not on your life*.

Chapter 8
Abit

DROWSINESS SWEPT OVER ME after that big lunch and long natter. I needed a nap. Back home, I took one most afternoons after a morning of woodworking and my midday dinner. Also I wasn't used to drinking so early in the day (though it was growing on me). I was heading up to my room when Nigel stopped me.

"We need to buy a car. I can't keep borrowing my friend's taxi. I know a good place over west of here, and I think you'd enjoy the ride."

We drove deep into the forest, where overhanging trees and hovering mist made it feel mysterious and dark, even though it was still afternoon. As Nigel took a sharp curve, I saw something shadowy up ahead. "Stop! Stop!" I shouted. He screeched to a halt, more out of shock than obeyance. Up ahead, I could just make out wild ponies off to the side of the road, bowing their heads to eat from the grassy verge. I'd had a magical encounter with wild ponies in Mt. Rogers park, back in Virginia, and seeing these some four thousand mile away gave me goosebumps. When I jumped outta the car, Nigel shouted for me to be careful. "They look like kiddie ponies," he said through the open car door, "but they're still wild animals."

I eased closer and talked to them while they munched. They paid me no nevermind, but I drank in their smell and big brown eyes. And beauty. Just like those back home, some were all black, others all white, or a mix with different colored patches. A few looked like small race horses with impossibly skinny legs holding up their wide bodies.

Nigel seemed to accept the situation; he didn't honk or hurry me along. I stood there a while longer and came to feel their natural calm, an authentic peace with themselves I wished I could find. The Mt. Rogers ponies had helped me see that it didn't matter where I was planted—in a good home or a mean one, in the mountains or a forest—I had a right to be what I was meant to be. That was also where, on a grassy meadow not unlike this one, I had embraced my true religion, one of my own making. Be kind. Simple words, hard to live up to, at least regular-like. But I kept trying.

"Come on, Abit. We need to get going," Nigel finally called out, his patience all but gone. I got back in and as we drove away, I rolled down my window and told those ponies I loved them. I didn't care what Nigel thought.

We rode along in silence and eventually came upon an encampment. There were tents and modern trailers, what the Brits call caravans, and a coupla bright wagons that reminded me of stagecoaches, only these were covered in painted curlicues and stars and horses in various poses. As I drank in this enchanted place, Nigel explained that these folks had come from Romania, most of them decades ago. In fact, their kinfolk had been in England since the fifteenth century, but even after all that time, people didn't much like them because they looked different and lived different. (Same thing back home. Outsiders kept that title forever.) They used to be called Gypsies because way back people thought they were from Egypt due to their dark coloring. These days they preferred Travellers, a name they got because they moved round a lot. Sometimes because they wanted to and other times because they were chased away.

"Now they mostly stay put," Nigel added. "Some folks are even helping them get 'pitching rights' so they can make more permanent homes." He saw me eyeing those fanciful wagons and added, "Their caravans are all pulled by trucks now." Okay, but as I studied them, I swear I could hear the old nags whinnying as they pulled the wagons somewhere new.

We drove a little farther and parked under some trees. When we got out, Nigel waved, and an older man walking our way waved back. As we got closer, Nigel said, "Silvanus, I'd like you to meet my friend Abit from the States. He's come to help us."

Silvanus took my hand and studied it, palm up and palm down. Then he smiled. "Welcome, young Abit. Is that your first name or last name?"

"First," I answered quickly, not wanting to get any further into that. We walked over to a dandy car—an old Morris Minor Nigel told me about on our way over. I hadn't heard of that kind of car before, but I did notice it sported some fine hubcaps. (That was oncet a pastime of mine.) The car was old but seemingly in great shape; even the red leather upholstery looked well cared for. Silvanus gave what sounded like a low price, and Nigel didn't bother to dicker.

"I need time to polish 'er up, so head over to Theodosia's for tea. I think she's been baking."

I couldn't believe we got to go to the very wagon I'd had my eye on. Outside, an ancient looking woman huddled over a fire where a kettle bubbled with steam. A dutch oven sat off to the side, scones cooling in the heavy black pan.

"Theodosia, it's Nigel, Nigel Steadman. Silvanus sent us over for tea."

When she looked up, her rheumy eyes couldn't have taken in much, but Nigel obviously meant something to her. A smile spread across her face as she stuck out her knobby hand, gnarled with arthritis and covered with rings that would never come off again without a saw. He took it in his, and I couldn't believe my eyes when he kissed it. Somehow she smiled even wider. Her hair was white, but her clothes ran through every color in the rainbow—swirls of red on folds of gauzy purple fabric, wide long sleeves that looked like they'd be a fire hazard, especially for a cook.

"Sit. Sit. And who is this with you?"

"Abit Bradshaw, from America," Nigel told her. "The mountains of North Carolina to be exact."

"Oh, mountains. How I miss my mountains. You are a lucky boy."

I didn't mind her calling me a boy—from her perspective I was one. I took her hand, but I didn't kiss it; I didn't reckon I was supposed to. We sat on a couple of wooden folding chairs painted bright blue. A feist ran over from some bushes, and the little feller sat near me so I could pet it. I couldn't stop myself from eying those scones, and even with poor eyesight, Theodosia didn't miss a thing. She reached over and took two from the pan, slathered them with butter from a striped bowl and handed one to each of us in the folds of a napkin. Steaming teacups followed.

Nigel knew just what to say, asking about her children and her arthritis. Come to think of it, that wasn't all that different from talking with old folks back home. I gave it a try and asked about a favorite in Laurel Falls—her garden.

"These old hands can still make turnip grow," she said, chuckling.

Not long after, Silvanus whistled for Nigel. We thanked Theodosia and headed toward the car. I got this feeling that comes over me sometimes; I reckoned you'd call it deep gratitude. I was touched by the hospitality she'd shared and wished I had something to give her for her kindness. I knew money wasn't the answer—it needed to be something that mattered to me. I stopped, even though Nigel was motioning for me to hurry, and took off my hat. Fastened on the brim was a pin I'd bought offa man at one of the festivals the Rollin' Ramblers played at. He'd had to explain to me it was cloisonné, which didn't mean much to me at the time. I just knew it caught the beauty of the mountains I called home: blue sky, purple mountains, green grass painted with fine glass, silver wires holding the colors in place till they were fired to a beautiful shine. I took it off my hat and walked back to Theodosia, placing it in her hand so she'd be sure to see it. I saw her holding it up close to her eyes as I trotted off to join Nigel.

Silvanus had the car running, and sure enough, he'd polished it and cleaned the windshield, or windscreen as he called it. It looked a treat all cleaned up and shining, and I couldn't wait to ride in it. Nigel gave him some bills and told him someone was coming soon to fetch the taxi parked under the trees.

On the way home Nigel's new car purred like a mountain lion—a little rough in spots, but all in all a fine purchase.

"THAT SCOUNDREL SWITCHED THE battery on me!"

Nigel had the Morris Minor's hood up, and I was looking on to see if I could help. We were stuck in a parking garage in Ringwood after buying supplies for the club's planned surveillance. (With any luck, I'd be back in Dublin by the time all that started.) Nigel discovered that what had been a bright new battery when we looked over the car before buying had been switched to an older one while we sipped tea with Theodosia.

I was surprised when Nigel burst out laughing.

"Wanker! I should've known he was up to no good. 'Polish 'er up,' my arse! Fortunately, we've got a crank. I bet you've never seen one of these, 'eh Abit? Though this won't exactly be inconspicuous on a stakeout. I'll see if Graham has an extra battery in his stash of old parts."

"Speaking of your arse, you've got glitter all over your britches," I called out.

"Cheeky bugger," he said, brushing his backside. "They love that stuff. And don't ask me why—I don't know!"

I was amused at first, watching Nigel turn red in the face trying to crank the motor. It was just like I'd seen in old pictures, sticking the crank in the front of the car and giving it a good turn. But when the red turned awful close to purple, I got out to help before he hurt himself. Between the two of us, we eventually heard the welcomed hum of the motor.

A Morris Minor is a small car, and my legs came in extra-long to hold up my six-foot-three frame. On the way home, I had to scooch round to get comfortable. Or try to. Nigel finally pulled up in front of the Bridgewater Arms.

I hurried off to my room, where I grabbed my phone to send Fiona and the boys an email. I was relieved I could get service in Lyndhurst because it was my only connection to them. I'd been gone just two days, but it felt a lot longer. I downplayed what Nigel had gotten me into and stuck with how much I liked my room at the inn and the good food. That would sound normal-like. Fiona wasn't as fond of Nigel as I was, maybe because he'd pulled me into his schemes before. She didn't write back. I figured she was off having fun with her family. As long as she had the boys with her, she seemed content without me.

THE PHONE WOULDN'T STOP ringing.

I'd fallen asleep, deep into some dream where I was running for my life. Not surprising, all things considered. When the phone kept ringing, I finally sensed it wasn't in my dream but in my hotel room. I grabbed it, all groggy and confused, and barked, "What?"

"Sir? Is this Mr. Bradshaw?"

"Er, yes. Sorry about that. What's up?"

"Nigel Steadman left you a message. It says here to grab dinner on your own. I might add we have a lovely special tonight with roast lamb, new potatoes, and fresh asparagus. You have just enough time for that before he picks you up around seven o'clock."

Man, that was some fine service, and I told him so. And fine by me to have dinner alone. Enough togetherness and running round for now. I put on a clean shirt, combed my hair, and went downstairs to the dining room. As was my custom, I said a little prayer of thanks to the lamb before plowing through the evening's special dinner. Then I asked the waitress about dessert.

"Oh, we have a fine pudding tonight, sir. Sherry trifle with fresh strawberries."

By the time I polished one of those off, I began to realize it probably hadn't been a great idea to drink a pint of lager with my dinner before our evening at the Dog & Bone. I ordered a coffee to sharpen my wits. The waiter brought over a thick ceramic cup with the name Rombouts painted across it. A brown cylinder with a white lid sat atop the cup. I peeked under the lid and saw hot water making its way through a filter. I'd been missing my perked coffee, and after doctoring it with cream and sugar, this coffee tasted close, maybe even better.

When Nigel pulled up to the Bridgewater Arms, I was waiting out front. He jumped out and told me to get in the driver's seat. "You need to get used to driving here," he said.

"Oh, you just want me to get glitter on my backside too." That made him laugh. I was feeling quite jovial after that fine dinner until it hit me he'd said I needed to *drive*. On the wrong side of the road. I hesitated, but he was already in the passenger seat. That made me think of my first-ever road trip with me driving, down near Staunton, Virginia. I clung to that steering wheel so hard my knuckles turned pure white—and
that was before I'd cranked the engine. But in the end I did it. And back then I was only nineteen year old, so what was my excuse now?

On the way over to the pub, we had time to talk. There wasn't much traffic, so I could concentrate on the left-hand side of the road and still carry on a conversation. I told him I'd help out with his plan this time, but that was it. No more debt, no more favors. "I'm not into this stuff like you are."

Nigel nodded. "You're a dreamer."

"No, I've got both feet on the ground, but I'm not as attached to the world as you are, what with you up to your elbows in money and deals and wrongdoings. My life is more like, oh, I don't know ... drifting in place. Reality is overrated."

"That doesn't make sense."

"It does to me, and that's all that matters."

Chapter 9
Della

WORKING WITH ANNIE TOTHEROW turned out to be more than I bargained for—in a good way.

When Mary Lou Dockery worked at Coburn's, she'd freed me up to do my ordering and get away from the store from time to time. Annie was different. Her depth of character drew me in, and the reporter in me wanted to know more. So naturally, I asked a lot of questions, the way reporters do, and she never hesitated with her answers. I learned how she was raised with four generations living together in one house and how her father, Elbert Totherow, my longtime source for sourwood honey, really was as kind as he appeared. It was difficult for me to imagine what it would be like to have a caring father, but the effect that had had on her stance in the world was obvious.

And she was great with customers. They responded to her, felt comfortable around her in a way they never did with me. Oh sure, I'd staked my claim in this town, and they now mostly accepted me (it only took twenty years!). Annie was a natural from the get-go.

We shared our lunches at least twice a week. Sometimes she even allowed herself to partake of reheated leftovers or something I'd whipped up before work. Folks around here can be slow to accept hospitality—even though they give of it freely. I remembered early on how I'd come home from visits laden with blackberries and canned tomatoes—even loaves of homemade bread. When I tried to reciprocate, I could sense their discomfort. Annie and I didn't allow that barrier to come between us.

"I remember coming to the store with Daddy when Abit's daddy owned it," she told me one day over a spicy gumbo made with lots of okra from my backyard garden. "I'd sit outside with Abit, who was usually leaning against the wall in his chair, sometimes all alone. Other times he'd be hanging out with all those old men. Daddy would come back out as fast as he could. He swore there were rats running round big as a house cat."

I shivered. "I believe I met a few of them when I first moved here. But don't feel too sorry for Abit. Those old men gave him something his father never could. Even when they didn't say much, like Wilkie Cartwright, they were sitting with him in a kind of solidarity."

As I got to know Annie better, she opened up more. It saddened me to learn that young women were still facing a lot of the same issues women my age had worked hard to change. (I'd naively hoped things were different now.) We shared experiences our respective generations struggled with: say you're sorry even when you haven't done anything wrong, don't take center stage, apologize for good ideas—anything to avoid being called nasty names just for being strong. It did sound as though things had gotten better, though sexual harassment still hovered over their lives. That was why Annie'd left the state's library system. Their loss. My gain.

And of course we talked about the customers. You had to let off steam or the job would drive you crazy. Like Fred Perotto, who was never satisfied. The ice cream was too creamy, the crackers were too crunchy. He was so contrary he became a running joke. When we'd sample a new cheese, for instance, one of us might say, "Oh, Fred wouldn't like this," referring to its luscious creaminess. Then there were the customers who'd tell us they wished the SuperMart out on the highway would open up in town. As though we'd be eager too—to have Coburn's put out of business.

The next day after I'd been upstairs going over the books for about the hundredth time, I looked at the clock and realized it was already eleven. Annie had opened for me, but I didn't want to leave her alone all morning. When I came through Coburn's front door, she looked close to tears. "Oh, no, did Fred come in today?" I asked.

"No, it was Mary Lou Dockery, of all people. She bought a whole bunch of groceries—apparently she's having a big family reunion—and I forgot to give her the special discount, which made her ..."

Annie's lip started to tremble. I jumped in. "All she had to do was ask for it, for crying out loud."

"Oh, she *did*. Then she told me she used to have my job, and she didn't forget things like that."

"So what? Stuff like that happens to everyone, and it's easily remedied. I'll have a talk with her and tell her I can take that discount away any time I want."

"Oh, no, ma'am. Please don't do that."

Ugh. *Ma'am*. I knew that came from her upbringing, but I hated being called ma'am. I'd hated it when I was forty, and I especially hated it now. But this was no time to lecture Annie about annoying nouns. "Okay, I won't say anything, but you let me know if she gets uppity again. She's probably got troubles at home, and a big reunion would put anyone on edge."

Annie nodded, but it felt more like she was just trying to let the topic drop.

ALEX CAME HOME THAT evening from a round of meetings over in Chapel Hill, where the magazine he managed was headquartered. The job took more time away from home than either of us expected (he'd agreed to work remotely from Laurel Falls, except for a *few* meetings), but it was a challenging job that called on all his talents. We'd been together off and on (mostly on) for a long time, but I still got excited when he returned to my life. His thick wavy hair had gone almost completely gray, but there was nothing colorless about the rest of him. Didn't hurt, either, that he'd brought Spaghetti alla Carbonara from a great Italian restaurant we'd discovered when I'd tagged along earlier in the year. He was carefully reheating it while I sipped a nice Pinot Grigio I'd brought up from the store.

"What have you heard from Abit?" Alex asked.

"I got an email that he'd had a good time in Dublin and was heading to England to visit with Nigel. I know he'll love seeing London."

"That sounds like a recipe for disaster—foreign country plus Nigel. Oh, and did I mention Nigel?"

"Okay, but I think after last summer Nigel has turned over a new leaf." I'd known Nigel Steadman almost as long as Alex. Back in D.C., I was working on a story about a white-collar crime ring, and someone connected me with Nigel, who'd agreed to help me, anonymously. He was under house arrest at the time for a complex forgery caper, and he was bored. Later he helped me with another series—after he'd flipped to work for the Treasury Department instead of driving them nuts with his nefarious expertise. And, of course, instead of going to prison. We'd stayed in touch ever since.

"He's turned that leaf over so many times, he probably can't tell which side he's on," Alex said.

I sighed. I guessed Nigel was an acquired taste. I loved him in spite of—and sometimes because of—his eccentric ways. Okay, not just eccentric. Illegal. But what was I doing pondering all *that* when I had Alex, wine, and Spaghetti alla Carbonara waiting? Oh, and toasted pistachio cannoli for dessert.

Chapter 10
Abit

OTHER THAN A FEW "LEFT, LEFT, LEFTs" from Nigel, I managed the drive on that side of the road just fine. We arrived at the Dog & Bone without a scratch. As I drove up to the pub, I was struck by all the handsome red brick with white woodwork, plus a chalkboard out front touting its specials. I'd never get a lick of work done back home if I'd had so many nice places to eat and drink.

I pulled into the carpark, proud I'd gotten us there without incident. As I started to cut the engine, Nigel grabbed my left arm. "First, leave the car running. Second, we need to talk." I waited for the bad news. Nigel musta seen the look on my face, because he laughed. "Hey, every time we talk doesn't mean something untoward is about to happen. I just wanted to explain how the evening's going to go and give you these pound notes to buy a round for the club and hopefully some of Clive's gang."

"I thought you said everyone knew your club members. What are *they* doing here?"

"I told you. Clive Ownbey and Ian McCafferty know *us*, but not that *you* know us. And it's only Roy Arthur and Marcia here tonight. They're not as well known. Just
enjoy yourself—listen to the music, scope out the scene, and with any luck, connect with McCafferty or one of Ownbey's other men."

"What will I say to them?"

"Oh, you'll figure it out. Roy will help you know who to talk to. Follow his lead. And if in doubt—make something up."

I'd met so many people I had to ask again which one was Roy. "You've got to be kidding, Abit. The musician? The guy wearing the boater? Roy Arthur Lewis?"

"Oh, yeah, right, right. The hat with the top cut out. Makes sense when it's hot out—I'll have to try that back home." Then it struck me it wasn't hot out. Oh, well, none of my business. "What instrument does Roy Arthur play?" I asked, but before the words were outta my mouth I remembered someone had called him a musician's musician. That surely meant more than one.

"Tonight should be fiddle," Nigel answered. "Or bass, your old instrument. What name did you give it? Beulah? Beatrice?"

That was one of the reasons I stayed friends with Nigel. He remembered things that others forgot, or never paid attention to in the first place. Of course, last summer he'd been to a gig or two of the Rollin' Ramblers while he stayed at our place, hiding from some other bad guys. But by then I played only the mandolin. I fell in love with the mando when Fiona gave me one that'd been in her family for years. Amazing he remembered ol' Bessie, my bass. And he was right. His mention of music did help my jitters.

"Now get your skates on and get out of the car before someone sees us together."

I got out, thinking about what lay ahead. "I guess I could say ..."

"Out, out, out," Nigel said, slipping over into the driver's seat and pulling away before I could ask anything else.

I WAS GLAD I'D been to enough pubs in D.C. and Dublin that I didn't feel like a complete rube. It helped that the inside of the Dog & Bone was so nice—even more than the outside. Old wood throughout, shiny with polish, and different colored bottles backlit in a way that made them glimmer. I spotted Roy Arthur straightaway. How could you not with that crazy hat? I headed his way and introduced myself. Kinda cloak and dagger, acting like we hadn't met before. We talked about music, and then someone told him it was time for the band to start. I headed to the bar to buy a pint and listen.

Like Nigel'd said, Roy Arthur played the fiddle, along with two other fiddlers, a guitar player, and a young woman on vocals. Her pretty voice filled the room as she put just the right pauses and inflections into the songs. The music was both new to me and familiar, not that different from the way our music back home sounded. Made sense given we'd mostly just put our own mark on Irish, English, and Scottish music.

After they played a while, and I'd downed a pint, I felt okay with how the evening was shaping up. I started to relax and looked round for someone to chat up. But then Roy Arthur stood and extended his fiddle toward me. "I just met a fellow from the States," he told the crowd, "and he says he plays the mando and bass. I didn't bring those instruments tonight, but maybe he can join us on the fiddle. I'll play my guitar for a while. What song do you want to play, Abit?"

I was so shocked I couldn't find my words. The crowd was looking at me funny—waiting for my answer. I got a sinking feeling they didn't like Americans all that much. This was *not* how Nigel said the evening would go. "Oh, they'll love you," he'd said out his window as he drove off. Yeah, love to run me outta town. But at that moment, I didn't have much choice. I needed to answer, so I blurted out the first thing that came to mind: "Well, I reckon we could play 'Red Haired Boy' in honor of my boy over in Ireland." But then I remembered then that they don't like the Irish either, but I plunged ahead. "I'm not so good on the fiddle, but I'll give it a go. Roy

Arthur here, I believe he could play a barbed wire fence if it were strung tight enough."

That brought the house down. I'd only said that out of nerves, but it broke the ice.

Fortunately the mando and fiddle are tuned the same, so I knew the notes. And Roy Arthur picked some I knew, like "Billy in the Lowground" and "June Apple." I didn't sound near as good as Fiona on the fiddle, but I held my own. My ears perked up when Roy Arthur leaned over to tell me he'd bring a mando for me tomorrow night. Just like that, I was in and set up for another night of music—and spying.

But all my bravado vanished when we took a break and Roy Arthur slipped away, leaving me standing alone at the bar. So much for helping me know who to talk to. For the longest time, I hung round like a sorry kid at a school dance. Then I got my chance.

Chapter 11
Abit

I spotted McCafferty (Roy Arthur had pointed him out earlier) going over to the bar to get a coupla pints. He stood tall as me and except for the collar-length curly black hair, looked the way most Brits look. He and another guy had been drinking together over by the fireplace, somewhere I was eager to get to. I wore a couple of layers of summer clothes, and even that wasn't enough (though I figured I'd look a right anorak wearing my coat indoors). While he waited for the publican to pull his pints, I stepped up and asked, "Do ya'll ever get warm days round here?"

I think it was the *ya'll* that got him, just like Nigel and the rest of the club had said. "Where are you from?" he asked, not friendly but not suspicious neither. When I told him, he seemed curious about what brought me to the New Forest. I was ready for him.

"I have family here. An elderly aunt who isn't doing all that well. She lives over near Lyndhurst, where I'm staying, but I wanted to try a different pub tonight. I heard about the music."

His drinking buddy came over to find out what the holdup was. We all introduced ourselves, and McCafferty told me to call him Ian. His friend Toby launched into more questions. *Where in America? Did I have a family? Were they here with me?* Things like that. He asked them so rapid fire I didn't have to give meaty answers, which was good because I didn't need that fireplace any more. I was sweating and hoped it didn't show.

As the two of them started trading friendly barbs and bits, this other-worldly feeling came over me, almost like a dream. I reckoned it stemmed, in part, from the fact that I'd actually made it to England, and here I was chatting with strangers (gangsters!) and carrying on like I knew what I was talking about. Their words faded, and I could only see them talking, sorta like Marcia's lip reading. It was as though we were all playing a big game, trying to best one another at every turn. It all seemed shallow, futile even. Like a peeing contest in the rain.

I was lost in thought when I felt Ian nudge me. "Earth to Abit. Earth to Abit."

"Oh, sorry," I mumbled. "Jetlag, you know. What did I miss?"

"You missed McCafferty making a rare request to get you something from the bar," Toby said, doing a bit of nudging himself. "Must be because Clive's out of town."

"That'd be nice," I said, trying to ease outta of my stupor. I perked up with that tidbit about Ownbey being out of town. "But only if you'll let me get the next round." He nodded, and I told him to choose something for me. I was stuck on Old Speckled Hen and wanted to branch out. He came back with Newcastle Brown Ale, and we stepped away from the bar so others could order.

Ian seemed like a nice enough guy, even though the club had warned me he was the wingman for Ownbey. I knew from talking with Nigel over the years that wingmen were more than followers; they looked out for the welfare of their boss. Maybe that meant I could get more information outta him, but it also meant he was more dangerous. Besides the fact that I didn't know what I was doing. That set me to worrying again, thinking about my boys and how I wished I'd just stayed home on the farm with Mollie and Della. Even Shiloh.

But here I was, and I needed to pull myself together. As long as I'd agreed to be part of this caper, I really wanted to find out something valuable for Nigel and his, well, whatever you'd call Nigella. Not sure how to do that, but I hoped I could get Ian's guard down, and he'd let something slip.

At first our conversation stuttered with a lot of stops and starts, but then he got on a tear about America. "My brother went over to hike the Appalachian Trail. Is that near you?"

"Comes close. About forty mile west but easy enough to get to."

"So how do you pronounce Appalachia? I've heard it at least a couple of ways."

"It's like 'I'm gonna throw an apple at cha.'" We politely chuckled over that, but then he and Toby started getting hepped up over politics and how greedy Americans were. And who could blame them for having the wrong impression, what with all the wars and bad headlines and stupid television shows they imported? I knew we'd thrown our weight round in the world, but I also knew we'd done some good. And that there were plenty of fine folks back home. I really didn't want to go down that road. Eventually, Toby threw me a lifesaver.

"Where'd that Southern accent come from? I mean, it's unique to your South, I believe. I can't think of anywhere else in the world where people talk like that."

At first I drew a blank—it was like asking someone why his face was round or his eyes blue—but then I remembered how some of our words still carried a hint of our British past. So I told him that and hammered it up a bit with more *reckons* and *young'uns* and *likes*. Toby seemed fascinated, but I could tell Ian was ready for the conversation to move on.

That's when he asked me what I did for a living. I could've just gone with the truth—woodworker and musician—but I heard

Nigel telling me to make stuff up. And to be honest, that sounded kinda fun.

"I'm a grocer. Got a chain of stores in the western part of North Carolina."

"Blimey, a young guy like you with a chain of stores?"

"Well," I said, looking down at my shoes in an aw-shucks kinda way, "my daddy was in the grocery business." (I'd always heard that to lie successfully you needed to stick close to the truth, and my daddy did own Coburn's oncet upon a time. Never mind he'd wrecked it before Della saved it.)

"Oh, so you inherited them?"

"You might say that. And I have a farm, though I've got help tending that." (Billy Bob Dockery came over with his hay mower twicet a year.)

"How much land you got?"

"About three hundred acres, give or take." (Mostly take.)

"What's that in hectares?"

"What're hectares?" That made them laugh. I wasn't sure why, but I figured laughter couldn't hurt.

"You got cattle, like those American ranchers we see on the telly?" Toby asked.

I could feel the sweat pouring down my hairline. Just when I was about to say I needed to move away from the fire, the musicians' break was over. Roy Arthur called me back on stage, and I played that fiddle like my life depended upon it. By the time we finished up with "Whiskey Before Breakfast," I was feeling a lot better. When the set broke, I moseyed over and got an Old Speckled Hen.

The bartender musta overheard our earlier talk, because while he sliced some lemons and limes, he told me three hundred acres was about the same as one hundred twenty hectares.

"How much is that worth in dollars?" he asked. I could tell he was the nosy type—with a red nose that looked like it'd been broken a few times. When he reached up to get a big bag of nuts for refilling the bowls on the bar, I noticed how ropy his arms were. Not someone I wanted to mess with.

"Good question," I hedged. "I don't rightly know. Prices just keep going up and up." His eyebrows went up too, and I felt ashamed of my lies, even though everything I said was true. I didn't know how much three hundred acres were worth, and the prices *were* always going up, thanks to all those second-home folks pouring into our county. He just nodded. If he only knew the truth—when you added up what I made and what I owed, you'd likely get a figure with a minus sign in front of it.

Roy Arthur walked over and congratulated me on my playing. He also slipped me a note that Nigel needed me to come out to the road, just past the carpark—and make sure I wasn't followed. I excused myself and said I needed to call it a night. Jetlag as an excuse was coming in handy.

Chapter 12
Abit

I GRABBED MY COAT and eased outta the pub, acting like I was just taking a walk to sober up. The wind had picked up and nearabout blew my hat off. I tucked it in my coat pocket as I snuck along a tall hedge. I spotted the Morris Minor off the road ahead. I tried to slip quietly into the passenger seat, but of course Nigel was sitting there because it was the driver's seat. I went round and sat to his left. "What's up?"

"Graham did some research into Ownbey's gang, and he thinks he knows one of the places they kip," Nigel said. "I want to get there before McCafferty or anyone else in the gang decides it's beddy-bye time." It was just after nine o'clock; I hoped we had enough time before the pub closed.

The lanes were so narrow I didn't know what drivers did if a car came from the other direction, but this time of evening, traffic was light. We came upon only one car, not far from a wide spot in the road. After a while, Nigel pulled off the lane onto a dirt track and slowly followed the path down toward a deserted-looking cottage in the middle of nowhere, tucked away so as no one would ever spot it from the road. We hadn't said a word since we left the pub.

I shoulda been scared, but to be honest, I'd always had a thing about looking in people's homes at night. Not like a Peeping Tom, up close and creepy. I just liked the glow from the windows, making things seem peaceful and pleasant. Even a dump like this one could make you think nice things were going on inside.

I could see recent tire marks, but no vehicles round the front. I told myself this was the kinda place a gang would stash their loot. I woulda laughed at myself for thinking thataway if the situation hadn't been so serious. I had *no* idea what a gang would do, but somehow this place seemed likely.

Nigel pulled over by some trees that gave us cover and kept the engine running. "Abit, just run along and have a butcher's (aka *look*)," he whispered, as if someone could hear us.

"Me? Why me?"

"You're young. I'll creak and groan heading over this uneven ground. I might even fall down. If you don't want to get caught with an old man tagging along behind you, just get out and have a look."

I knew that was part truth and part convenience talking, but I eased outta the car and hugged the trees as I made my way closer to the cottage. As if I weren't nervous enough, a heavy mist painted everything with an eerie glow; I halfway expected to see a haint hovering over the house. I got a shiver from the wind, though I hoped that would work in my favor. Any little noises I made would be covered by the sounds of the wind blowing things round.

And I'd no sooner thought that than a gust of wind broke a limb not far from me. I think I let out a little yelp, something you can't help when you're scared. And I *was* scared. I waited to make sure no one came outside before I snuck up to the window next to the lighted one. That way, I figured, I ran less risk of coming face to face with a gangster looking out to see what was going on. I could see someone sitting on the couch, but he was snoring loud enough to hear it through the closed window.

When another gust of wind caused a branch to knock against the house, the man woke up with one of those "Huh? What? Where am I?" reactions, but he got his wits about him quick-like and ran over to the window nearest him. I crouched down below my window and held my breath. After what felt like an eternity, I could see the light get brighter when he quit blocking it and went back to his couch. I knew from that he was a big guy.

Then I started worrying he might be coming outside for a better look. I eased toward the backside of the cottage and waited. Eventually I felt it was safe to work my way round the rest of the cottage, cupping my hands to help me see in each window. Some were too dark; others had just enough light creeping in for me to see some old furniture and crap piled up. I did catch a glimpse of something shiny and new in one corner, but I couldn't get a good angle on it. On the way back to the car, I also saw a shed behind the house with a big padlock on it.

When I was finally inside the car, Nigel pulled forward slowly, easing over the dirt track. It wasn't till we were on the paved lane that he put his foot down hard on the accelerator; by then it was dark enough to need the headlights. When I finally spoke, Nigel flinched, the sound of my voice breaking through the quiet. "I didn't see much other than someone sleeping on the couch and a shed with a padlock."

"Well, that's how it goes in this business, Abit."

"I know, but I wanted to find something."

"You need to learn that ..."

"No, I *don't* need to learn," I shot back. I felt my fear and anger meld into a fury that surprised even me. I couldn't believe he wanted to lecture me on how to be good at this kind of life. "This is the last time I'm doing anything crazy like this. One more night, Nigel. One more night."

"We'll see," he said, as if I were a prisoner with no free will. We rode along stone silent till he said, "Give me two, old chap. Just two more?"

As we approached the Dog & Bone, Nigel pulled off in his hiding place. "I did see something new in that ramshackle place," I told him. "but I couldn't quite tell what it was. And now that I've had time to think on it, that guy couldn't have been living there. It wasn't set up like a home or anything like that. More like a hideout."

"That's a good lad," he said. And without thinking about it, he shut the engine off. The minute he did, we both knew he'd forgotten about the dodgy battery. He tried to start it again. Nothing.

"Well, now we'll have to crank it." I could tell he expected me to do it, but he'd gotten into this mess all on his own, so he could at least try. He gave it a few turns, but no luck. If I didn't want to spend all night there, or take him to the emergency room, I reckoned I'd better help.

After five or six tries with the crank, we heard the engine sputter and level out to a surprisingly healthy purr. "You'll just have to learn, Nigel," I parroted, "... not to turn the engine off!"

As I got out, he was saying something about seeing me back at the Bridgewater Arms. I waved him off and walked toward the pub. I still had a half hour before last call to try to get information out of someone. I was surprised to see Ian standing at the bar, chatting with the nosy bartender.

"Oh, there you are, Abit. I thought you'd gone for the evening," Ian said, all friendly-like. "Did you need to check on your grocery monopoly in Laurel Falls, North Carolina?"

Something scared me about his tone—and the fact he knew the name of our small town. Had he been checking up on me? Surely I wasn't that bad an actor. But then I figured there was no way he could know I didn't own the SuperMart or any number of grocery stores back home. Or even if he found out I was a lying fool, so what? Wouldn't he just think I was a blowhard? He and Toby already thought that about Americans anyway.

I looked at my watch. "Well, the stores are still open, given the time difference, but no, I'm on vacation. I'd planned to head back to my inn, but then I asked myself how many nights do I get to spend in England? I can sleep back home."

"Well, you played a fine fiddle tonight. I was surprised when Roy Arthur said it wasn't your preferred instrument." We talked a while about traditional music, both here and in the States. And then he said something kinda strange. "I envy you."

I nearly choked on my beer. Abit Bradshaw, the laughing stock of Laurel Falls when I was growing up, a humble craftsman and musician who mostly hid out on a nine-acre farm. The only thing I could imagine he'd envy was my family: lovely Fiona, two fine boys, and Mollie. But we hadn't talked about family. Of course, he thought I was well-to-do, so that was likely it. I swallowed hard and put my pint down. "Now why would that be, Ian?"

"You seem settled in yourself. Me? I don't fancy what I do. It's time to make a change."

"So how do you make a living, Ian?"

He shot me a look with such darkness, I had to turn away. Then the last-call bell rang, and the barman gave the shout. Several customers crowded the bar, and the spell was broken.

"Well, Abit, just in time," Ian said, his awkwardness smoothed over. "Meet my friends, Reggie and Stanley." I nodded and tried to act normal-like. "Abit here is a Renaissance man from North Carolina. He plays music, runs a farm, and heads up a grocery chain. And he doesn't even have a wrinkle or receding hairline yet."

I was taken aback by the change in his tone. Gone was the dark, electric feeling I got just a minute ago. Until then, he'd mostly come across polished and, well, nice. Then I got a flash of something deeper inside him. I wasn't a fool—I knew he had his cards to play too, but I hoped he didn't know we were both playing a game. The two men nodded my way and I said, with my strongest Southern accent, "Nice to meet you boys."

For some reason that cracked them up. At the time I thought it was my accent again, but later I'd come to understand they thought it was funny anyone thought it was nice to meet them.

FOLKS STARTED LEAVING THE pub, the bartender bidding them goodnight while he polished the brass on the beer taps and closed down the bar. The evening had overwhelmed me with too many drinks, lies, and strangers. I felt a rush of gratitude when Roy Arthur came over and said he was going my way, could he give me a ride home? Nigel had probably arranged that to keep our cover—just a helpful guy saving me cab fare. Roy Arthur leaned over and asked Ian if he'd be there the next night. "You won't want to miss Abit on the mando!" Then he slapped me on the back so hard I stumbled. Everyone laughed, and that time I knew they *were* laughing at me.

We didn't say much on the way back to Bridgewater Arms, though I did ask him why he'd slapped me so hard.

"Oh, just part of the banter and play acting, I guess. Sorry. Did I hurt you?"

I wasn't about to admit that it wasn't my back he'd hurt but my feelings. I just shook my head. I was tired and glad I wasn't driving after so much beer. I didn't usually drink that much, but I'd thought it would help with my nerves and give me something to do with my hands. When we got back to the hotel, I was surprised Roy followed me up to my room, where Marcia, Graham, and Nigel were waiting.

I couldn't get away from them!

Chapter 13
Della

THE MYSTERY OF THE shrinking inventory persisted, even with close scrutiny of the ledgers. I needed help, but this wasn't the kind of problem I could take to the sheriff. Especially the one we had. I'd worked with Sheriff Horne before, and he was good at what he did—as long as it landed in his lap. Anything requiring much initiative was a different story.

I'd tried to do what I could on my own. A few weeks ago, even before I met with the forensic accountant, I'd installed a couple of cameras high up in the store, disguising them by hollowing out two old speakers and inserting the cameras. I didn't want them sticking out. Even though CCTV was everywhere now in big cities and around the world, Laurel Falls customers would leave in droves if they thought they were being recorded.

The *idea* of capturing the thief on camera fired up my reporterly zeal, but the *reality* of reviewing all those recordings filled me with dread. Back in the day, I'd watched more footage than Steven Spielberg, eager to find crooks and build my career. It had been a wild ride filled with adrenaline and even danger, which suited me then. Looking back, I realized I hadn't become a reporter so much because I yearned to be a journalist as it was a good fit for my personality. I got to roam D.C. and be my naturally bossy, brassy self. Confrontation was a good thing, unlike any other job I could think of, especially the ones back then that society deemed suitable jobs for women. But now? I just wanted to find this thief and get back to the life I'd carved out here.

I decided not to burden Annie with all this. She was too new on the job and too innocent; she'd be horrified if she saw one of her neighbors or even a family member doing something wrong. But that all changed later that week when she came upstairs to tell me a customer wanted to see me. (Fred Perotto complaining the jam was too chunky with fruit.) She looked startled when she caught me watching the surveillance videos. Not because she could see my screen, but because I slammed my laptop shut, like a teenager caught binge-watching lurid videos. It was lurid, all right, in such a depressing way.

I didn't say anything at the time. I just headed downstairs, told Fred to buy jelly next time, and went about my storekeeping business. Later, after I'd been through all the videos to date and was starting to go cross-eyed, I decided Annie and I were working as a team, and she needed to know. The next evening I asked if she could stay late, just for an hour or so after we closed.

"Happily. I love my family, but all those Totherows under one roof get old after a while.," she said.

"Do you have your old room back?" I asked, recalling that time when Abit was just a teenager and we'd stopped by for honey. He walked past her room—all pink and pretty—and had one of those flashbulb moments. I believe twenty years later he could describe it in detail. No need to tell her that, though.

"No," she answered. "Real estate in that house is too valuable for sentimentality. When I went off to college and lived in Raleigh for a few years, my sister and her baby took over that room. I have my own place in the honey room."

"With all the bees?"

Annie giggled, putting her hand to her mouth to hide how ridiculous my question was. "No, ma'am. They stay outside. It's a room offa where Daddy and I extract the honey. It smells great. And best of all, it's private."

I joined her in laughing at my stupid question, which felt good. We both needed a little mirth given what I was about to reveal after we closed the store.

Of course Winnie Ivester came in at the last minute and stayed a good fifteen minutes after our six o'clock closing. At least she had the good grace to spend some real money. When we pulled the shade and locked the door, we both did our end-of-the-day duties. Then I opened a bottle of Malbec I was particularly fond of.

"Do you drink wine, Annie?"

"When I'm not at home," she said, a big smile across her freckled face. I knew her family was the teetotaling type.

"Good. Let's go in the back and have a glass of wine. I'll explain what this is all about." I didn't waste any time. I knew how women like Annie thought—that I was laying her off or about to lecture her for some alleged wrongdoing.

Ten minutes later she came into the back. "I think I did everything right, ma'am."

Okay, I'd had enough; first things first. "Have a seat, ma'am," I said and poured her a glass of wine. "Oh, and help yourself to some cheeses, ma'am. I thought we'd sample a new one—mimolette. It's a hard cheese originally inspired by the Dutch Edam cheese, ma'am."

She sat down, picked up her wine, and gave me the strangest look. Then she burst out laughing. "I take it you don't want me calling you *ma'am* anymore."

Ah, my kind of gal. "Doesn't feel so good, does it?"

"No, ma'am," she said, chuckling.

We chatted a while and ate the cheeses—I liked the mimolette, but Annie found it too dry. (Fred Perotto would have loved it.) We both liked the morbier and the wine.

"Listen, Annie, you're doing a great job."

"But not good enough?"

"I knew it! I should have told you straight away this wasn't about your performance. No, I couldn't be more pleased. This meeting is about finding the person who is robbing us blind."

"Oh, I hope you don't think it's me!"

Honestly. What do we do to young women to make them so self-effacing? I remember being the same way. Well, maybe not me so much, but my friends. And there it was again—that feeling that things hadn't changed as much as I'd hoped. Or maybe it just takes longer to unpack cultural baggage than I had the patience for.

"Okay, let's start over. You're doing a great job, I know you aren't stealing from me, and I trust you enough to bring you in on what's going on." She let out a sigh of relief. Finally, we seemed to be on the same wavelength. "I've installed some cameras. Have you noticed them in the corners up high?"

"Oh, that's what those things are. I thought they were speakers. But now that you mention it, you don't play music."

"Yeah, I like Coburn's to be a noise-free zone—other than people talking to one another. I used some old speakers to help disguise the cameras. Guess it worked."

"Have you found out anything? What kind of videos do you have—and where to you watch them?" Her face brightened. "Oh, that's what you were watching the other day when I came upstairs!" Again, relief.

I laughed. "Yes—and no, it wasn't porn." Her red face confirmed my suspicions. Then we got down to the more technical stuff. Being a librarian involved a lot more than shelving and checking out books. Annie was a whiz on the internet and with what we used to call audio/visuals.

I showed her the videos, and we reviewed that day's together. I hated what all this thieving had done to the way I looked at my customers. Everyone was a suspect, even my favorites. I had to smile when we caught Cleva Hall walking out eating cookies without paying for them. She had been my best friend for twenty years, even though I no longer saw her as much as I once did. Over the years, she'd been that extra person in my life, the one who listened, cared, and even admonished—but always with my best in mind. Now almost ninety, she lived near her niece, who'd brought her in to shop and didn't realize the cookies hadn't been paid for. I owed Cleva so much, she could pull a truck up to the store and clean me out, and we still wouldn't be close to even.

Annie and I were both tired from a long day, so I shut down the laptop and locked the front door as we left the store. When she got to her car, Annie turned and called out: "What have you heard from Abit?"

"He's having fun, I think. He was in Dublin, but now I think he's in London. Sounds wonderful, doesn't it?"

Chapter 14

Abit

"DID YOU GET TO TALK with Clive?" Nigel blurted out as soon as Roy Arthur and I walked into my room. No niceties anymore. All business, *his* kind of business.

It irked me that I was getting grilled before I could take my coat off. "No he's traveling, according to Toby."

"Who's Toby?"

I explained he was Ian's sidekick, and then I asked Nigel if he knew Clive Ownbey personally.

"Everyone knows him, Abit. He's a bad dude, as they say in the States, so be careful."

That irked me too, as though this caper was *my* problem. I grumbled something to that effect, and Marcia and Roy Arthur tittered at my ornery reply. Nigel just shrugged.

"Well, considering he's out of town," I said, "I should be safe."

"Except his wingman McCafferty can be just as bad," Roy Arthur chimed in. "And I believe I've heard tales about that bloke Toby."

"Yeah, he and Ian are right chancers," Graham added. "They'll take advantage of a rube like you and run with it."

Everyone flinched when Nigel jumped up and grabbed Graham's chair, giving it a shake. "What did you just say?"

"Uh, I don't know, mate. Something about McCafferty being a chancer?"

"You should have stopped with that," Nigel spat. "How dare you speak to Abit that way! Have you lost all your manners in that wretched computer world you live in?"

I was so used to it, I hadn't even realized I'd been insulted. I felt my face going red, and when I glanced over at Graham, his was too. Even though Nigel'd irritated me daily on this trip, I had to admit he looked out for me—whether I was belittling myself or someone else was having a go at me. Like how he took on Johnny Ray Meeks last summer. Nigel could talk rough to me sometimes, shout at me before I could take my coat off, but when it was all said and done, I knew he was my friend.

Nigel let go of Graham's chair and cleared his throat. Graham nodded an apology, and I nodded back. The British way.

"Er, I'm glad I didn't know all this earlier," I said to move things along. "Toby seemed kinda stupid, but Ian had a way about him. What's he done?"

Nigel answered. "He's been detained at Her Majesty's pleasure three times that we know of—for robbery and racketeering."

"I used to hang out with Ian," Marcia said, her voice tender-like. "He wasn't so bad when we were younger. He's still got his good looks and his manners, but I know he's gotten himself into some bad things. After that last stretch in prison, he told me he wanted to go straight, but now he's in with Ownbey. I can't figure that." She thought for a moment. "You need to be careful, Abit. But you did good. We know Clive is away, and Ian is running things for now—and he's a great contact to have. Tomorrow night you can find out more."

That wasn't exactly the bedtime story I needed. I tossed and turned all night.

Chapter 15
Abit

"How's that full English?" Nigel asked, sipping his coffee.

The next morning Nigel came by for breakfast. He was in a better mood than the night before, so things went more like old times.

For a guy his size, he didn't eat much. I reckoned he was worried about Nigella, but I wasn't. I plowed into my plateful of eggs over easy, bangers, bacon, Heinz beans, fried bread, grilled tomatoes, and mushrooms. And toast and marmalade. Even I found all that pretty outrageous, but I loved every bite.

I asked about his grandsons, especially Jason who'd come down to clear out all the stuff Nigel left in our guestroom last summer after he'd had to flee the country so sudden-like. Nigel asked about the guy who'd killed three people in the North Carolina mountains. He'd left right in the middle of all that, and Della must not have given him the news. Probably couldn't find him with all his moving round. I filled him in and explained how Vern came to live with us.

He nodded his approval when I told him Conor now had a little brother.

"Well, we need to take good care of you so you can get home to them safely," he said like the King of England making a declaration. I knew he thought that was reassuring, but he was the one who'd dragged me into this mess.

"What are they known for?" I asked.

"Who?"

"Clive Ownbey's gang—what are they known for?"

"Known for?"

I sighed. Why was he being so difficult? Of course I knew he was hedging so he could come up with an answer that didn't send me running for the ferry back to Ireland. "Come on, Nigel. What has this gang done in the past? Robberies?"

"Yes, I believe that's obvious, what with Nigella and all."

"Okay, anything else?"

"Well, um, some embezzlement and, and ..."

"And murder? You don't want to say it, but I'm right, aren't I? It's murder, isn't it?"

"Not that they were ever charged, mind you."

"Yes, I *do* mind. Tell me about it."

And he did. An awful story that sounded like a bad TV show with mobsters and watery graves and such. "And you want me to hang out with these types? ON MY VACATION?"

"Oh, come on, boyo. You're just standing in a pub talking to a few of them."

"And peeping in windows at one of their hideouts and no telling what else you have in mind. Well, just for the record, I'll talk to Ian one more evening and that's it."

Nigel nodded, looking kinda sad. I'd like to think he felt bad about what he was asking of me, but I think it was really about me not being round to help with his dirty work.

After paying the tab, Nigel let me know he'd be out the rest of the day, but we'd have dinner together. That arrangement suited me fine. I had the day to myself and could putter round my room. I went upstairs and made myself a cuppa with the tea service the maid had replenished earlier.

I hadn't planned on traveling on my own, but no way was I going to sit in my room all day and read dog-eared copies of "Women & Home" or "Woman's Own" left behind by previous guests. I wished someone like Marcia or Roy Arthur would show me the sights. I had a dim memory of Nigel saying someone was going to take me to Stonehenge; I sure wanted to see those stones. But then I remembered we weren't supposed to be seen together.

I'd kept it to myself that my thirty-seventh birthday was coming up in a few days. I'd overheard my family making plans for when I returned to Dublin, and I counted on being back in time for that. But it was my habit to milk the week *before* my birthday for all the extra attention and favors I could muster. I guessed I'd have to do that for myself.

I walked into Lyndhurst and treated myself to a scone and a double latte at the kind of teashop Fiona loved. And missed. Back in Laurel Falls, she longed for a lot of things. Like how nice the towns in Ireland look. Laurel Falls reminded me more of a Hollywood set for a wore out Western town, and I knew Fiona agreed. Empty storefronts, dusty roads, world-weary people. Lyndhurst was just the opposite. Hanging baskets overflowing with bright flowers, tearooms chockful of cakes, stores filled with knitted sweaters, homemade jams, and local honeys. Everything spoke of pride in their local ways.

To be fair, we had nice things back home—handmade quilts and woodcarvings, homemade jams and relishes, but we thought of all that as just things we'd made to get by. Nowadays, of course, Della sold a lot of that to tourists, so I guessed some folks did see the treasure we had right in our own hometown. That got me thinking about Annie Totherow. She and her father used to deliver honey to Coburn's when Daddy owned it. Oncet Annie went away to work somewhere in the eastern part of the state, Elbert brought it by on his own—or sometimes he got Della to come pick it up.

Annie was my first sorta girlfriend, though she never knew a thing about that. I just carried those feelings inside, figuring she'd laugh in my face if I'd've said anything about how much I liked her. Fiona was my only real girlfriend, and it surprised me to this day that she took to me, especially back then when I was all legs and nerves.

As I walked through Lyndhurst, I thought about how much I'd like to see Laurel Falls all fixed up nice. Not like that town down in Georgia that made itself into an Alpine village. Things there had gotten so carried away it'd turned into a tourist trap. But I had to hand it to those local folks. When they first started up, they really came together to make a better life for themselves. It wasn't till they made it a success that all the Disney-type suits came in and turned it into a spectacle. I just wished we took more pride in our town for our own sake.

Lyndhurst was jammed with people, so I was happy to be on foot. I carried my coffee and scone up the high street to the parish church, St. Michael and All Angels. I found a spot on the grass and settled in with a brochure I'd picked up. I was lucky with the weather. The cold bluster had calmed down, though thick clouds still skuttled across the sky, opening up now and then to bits of blue sky, something Fiona called Dutchman's britches. "Enough blue sky to make a pair of Dutchman's britches," she'd say, and the boys would laugh. Back home we usually had enough blue sky to clothe every man in Holland, but in Ireland and here in England, I'd come to realize it was important to make the most of bright intervals.

I sat down and leaned against a tree with smooth bark and read that the parish church was actually fairly recent—nineteenth century, which in this country is next to brand new—but older churches had been on this very spot. I wandered inside to see the windows William Morris designed. I'd learned about his work at The Hicks, where we studied the Arts & Crafts Movement, both in America and England. Before now I'd seen his designs only as pictures in books; oncet I saw the real thing, I felt a rush of renewed admiration.

I went back outside and walked round the church's cemetery where I found the gravestone for Alice Pleasance Liddell, the young girl who'd inspired Lewis Carroll's *Alice's Adventures in Wonderland* and *Through the Looking Glass.* The stone used her married name, Mrs. Reginal Hargreaves, in the way they did not all that long ago. I couldn't believe how much interesting history was packed into this small island.

I passed some thatched cottages (a craft I'd love to see in action) so charming I had to stop and stare. After a bit, someone came out her front door, and I took off, thinking she was about to tell me to get a move on. But as I turned away, I saw her smile and wave. Things were different here than back home.

Before long I was deep in the forest, where I came across more ponies. Of course, they didn't give me the time of day, their attention fixed on munching. I saw birds I didn't know the names of and some I did, like the crow and kestrel. I'd later discover in my guidebook that I'd also seen a stonechat and bluetit. I walked over the heath, then crossed a bridge, and eventually entered a wooded area with oak trees so grand it was no wonder the Druids worshiped them. I smelled wood smoke as I walked, drifting from an unseen cottage, no doubt. Looking at all the old, gnarly trees, I wondered how they felt about their kinfolk being burned up, right under their noses. But they'd been round for centuries, so I guessed they were used to it.

It was there, in the quiet of the forest, that a notion came upon me about Nigel's situation. I'd have to talk with him about it at dinner.

I was beginning to feel lost when a path appeared that led to the high street. It felt good to recognize my surroundings. I didn't know it then, but in a day or two, I'd have no idea where I was.

Chapter 16
Abit

BEFORE HEADING UP TO MY ROOM, I bought a golden-browned Cornish pastie for my lunch, which I figured would go perfectly with a cuppa I could make in my room. I'd decided to skip a more formal lunch because my money was running tight (along with my waistband).

I was looking forward to having a quiet lunch, but when I opened the door to my room, I sensed something wasn't right. It wasn't all tore up, but I could tell things weren't the way I'd left them. I tried to convince myself it was the housekeeper, but my bed wasn't made yet and the towels were still damp from my morning shave. I walked round the room and noticed the mattress was slightly off its frame and a dresser drawer was open about an inch. I'm funny that way—I wouldn't've left things like that. I righted everything and checked my suitcase for my passport. It was in there, but not in the same place I'd stashed it. I put it and my extra money in my jacket pocket.

I decided not to mention it to the hotel manager because I didn't really have any proof. Besides, it had to be Clive Ownbey's boys, maybe even Ian, which made the idea of talking with him that night even more troubling. Whoever did it, though, hadn't gained much information about me—other than getting the wrong idea about me reading "Woman's Own."

I didn't want my pastie to go to waste, so I set it out on a napkin and stepped over to make myself a cuppa. That was when a wave of fear washed over me. Fiona's picture—the one with the boys and Mollie I'd brought special for this trip—was lying on the tea table. Some scoundrel had taken it out of the drawer and set it where I'd be sure to see it. I sat down at the table and held the picture close.

Somehow I managed to eat my lunch, and I musta drifted off because heavy knocking on my door roused me, intruding on a dream I was enjoying about Mollie. She'd come with me on this trip and was entertaining people in the pub with her antics and good looks. It was great to see her again, and I resented our visit being cut short.

I jumped up and pulled the door open. The front desk woman—Cilla, I believe she'd told me earlier—held a message out to me. I wasn't sure if I was supposed to tip her, but I couldn't find any coins. She smiled. "Buy me a drink tonight when I get off duty," she said, then slipped away. I wasn't sure what to make of that.

The note was from, who else, Nigel. *Dinner 6pm sharp!* You'd've thought it was a telegram and he was paying for every word. Nothing about what the all-fired important meeting was about. I stretched and thought about how after that light lunch and long walk, I'd be ready.

WHEN I ENTERED THE backroom, the club members were already there, clustered round the table. After we ordered dinner (shepherd's pie for me), Nigel brought everyone up to date with what I'd discovered last night and what he'd just found out. He'd spent the day casing the same cottage we'd been to and saw a couple of men coming and going with boxes that looked light going in and heavy coming out.

"We can't jump to conclusions about that ..." Nigel started to say before Marcia interrupted him.

"Oh, er, if you don't mind, I have something to contribute. I would have shared this last night, but I couldn't find my reading glasses. While Abit was talking with Ian last night, you might recall that Toby joined them? Well, when Abit went to buy a round, they were talking and they said ... hang on a minute, let me check my notes ... that Clive had found the right man, and they'd be moving it all out tomorrow night—which would be tonight."

"Good lord, Marcia! What would we do without you?" Nigel said, beaming at her. Then he turned to me. "Let's build on that this evening, Abit. Nigella's hearing is coming up, and we need something more than 'I didn't do it.'"

Easy for you to say, I thought as I looked round at everyone. They all seemed happy with the new information, but it wasn't enough for me. "Okay, but how do we know they're referring to the jewelry that got Nigella into trouble? They could be talking about whiskey or gold bullion, for all we know." I was sorry to knock the wind outta their sails, but I couldn't be putting myself in danger for a caper that wasn't related to Nigel's. And as much as I hated to drag out this investigation, I wanted to share my other notion with them as well. "Another thing. Do you think we're making a mistake looking only at Ownbey and his gang? We're running in a straight line toward them, but it might take us right off a cliff."

Nigel sat quiet-like for a moment, like he was arguing with himself over what I'd just said. "I hate to admit it, but Abit's right. We've got tunnel vision. Graham, could you and Alfred have a look into that other gang down in Bournemouth? I don't want to go on halfcocked. And any others you can find. I was certain Ownbey was dealing with jewelry, but these gangs are creating misery in all kinds of ways." He rubbed his chin a bit and then added,

"Graham, get back to us by tomorrow or the next day, all right?"

Graham got up and left, apparently to get to work on the new angle. But none of this changed the task facing me that evening. "If any of you have an idea about what I can ask tonight," I said, "I'm all ears." They chuckled. I blushed. I'd been kidded about my big ears before, and I wished I'd used a different saying. "If I'm going to help you, I need to do it tonight."

They all nodded; I figured Nigel had filled them in on my situation. "Did you ask McCafferty what kind of work he did?" Graham asked. "I'd love to hear how he responds to that!"

"Me too. And whatever they've got going on tonight, Ian will likely leave early." That was Marcia again. "Ask him where he's headed."

There were a few other suggestions, and I finally knew what I needed to do.

Chapter 17
Della

"WE'LL CATCH THE SCOUNDRELS, Della. I promise."

Alex was trying to cheer me up on our trip home from Asheville. We'd had a lovely walk and dinner in town, but I couldn't shake the depressing report from the forensic accountant. Before this trip, I hadn't asked Alex to get involved—he'd been too busy with his own work—but now, the way things were going, I'd take all the help I could get. Once I figured out what that even meant.

We'd had a good ride down the mountain to Asheville, talking about things we were often too rushed to share. Nothing big like the state of the world—more like who his most supportive staff members were and where he was sending them on assignment. I told him about some new products in the store, like rum raisin chocolate bars from Germany and Mrs. Poindexter's homemade hand pies and zucchini lasagna entrees. (I'd finally caught up with the times. People weren't cooking as much these days, even out here in the country, which opened new markets for frozen entrees from enterprising cooks working through the community kitchen.)

We'd decided to get the dreaded accountant appointment over with first and save the fun things for afterwards. As I'd feared, she'd reviewed the additional files I'd emailed her and reported that the thefts were getting worse. She showed us a report that made it very clear that Coburn's would be in serious financial trouble by autumn if we didn't stop the culprits. Of course, she only put the official stamp on what I already knew, but something about her grim face and undertaker-ish voice made the news doubly hard to take.

We'd remembered to bring sensible shoes for a leisurely walk afterwards. We lived in the mountains, so we weren't looking for a long hike. Riverside Cemetery fit the bill. With its shady acreage bedecked with Victorian mausoleums and obelisks, it is a remarkably welcoming place, all things considered. For some reason I'd felt the need to dress up for the accountant, likely to prove I was as professional as she was, not some lamebrain getting royally ripped off, so we looked a little overdressed walking around the grounds. *Then again*, I thought, *maybe we just looked like people attending a funeral*. Which, in a way, we were. Coburn's.

I tried to put all that behind me as we strolled through the rolling, green hills. I'd been there before for a Thomas Wolfe birthday party, so I showed Alex where his grave was. We offered our respects before heading over to the tombstone of O. Henry, aka William Sydney Porter. He'd kept an office in downtown Asheville for a few months toward the end of his short life, a writer's garret I'd enjoyed walking past over the years, thinking of the fine storytelling that had gone on inside. As we approached his stone, we noted a pile of pennies scattered on top, an ongoing gift from readers in honor of the opening line of "The Gift of the Magi." *One dollar and eighty-seven cents. That was all. And sixty cents of it was in pennies.* Apparently the money is collected every year and donated to the local library. We both dug into our pockets for coins.

We walked quietly until I heard Alex's stomach growl; mine followed like an echo. We both laughed and admitted we'd been thinking about a white-tablecloth dinner all day (and the day before for me). We chose a new restaurant on the downtown square: Persimmon. It was pretty inside, but so posh I felt a little uncomfortable. White-tablecloth is one thing; this was quite another.

When I'd first moved to North Carolina, Asheville was a place better known for its meat-and-three cafés. Some of the best I ever had, with hard-working waitstaff shouting out orders and cutting into mile-high pie (think extreme meringue topping). As much as I enjoyed well-prepared food, I lamented how trendy Asheville had become. I knew from my customers that their friends and family living down there were struggling with higher taxes, real estate prices through the roof, and everyday items harder and harder to find in town.

We decided to leave and go somewhere less pretentious. Just down Biltmore Avenue we found a cozy little place, though we hoped the menu was more creative than its name: The Bistro. It was. Alex was feeling flush from a good run with the magazine and told me to get anything I wanted; dinner was on him. I knew his offer had more than a dollop of pity following the accountant's report, but I wouldn't let that get between me and a kind gift—and a good meal. Besides, I would have done the same for him.

I ordered seared rainbow trout with swiss chard and wild rice. Alex got the short ribs with grilled asparagus and sugar snap peas. Beer sounded better than wine for both of us, and the waiter suggested a local craft-brewed lager. We split a rhubarb crumble with housemade vanilla ice cream. A French press of coffee helped get us home.

I felt so contented, I couldn't imagine anything untoward reaching our door ever again.

Chapter 18
Abit

THAT EVENING, ROY ARTHUR begged off driving me to the Dog & Bone, so Nigel took me, dropping me a good ways from the front door.

"I wish we could have a pint together," I said before closing the car door.

"It's better this way, boyo. Can't let them see us together. And, er, well..."

I got kinda scared. He had this look on his face like he was about to tell me some bad news. "Are you okay, Nigel?"

"Better than ever, Abit. Just that I've had to give up the sink." When I looked at him funny, he laughed. "You know the *kitchen sink*, Cockney rhyme with *drink?* Lots of reasons, not the least of which is I need me wits about me to spring Nigella."

I figured it was more serious than that, but I let it go.

As I walked toward the front door, I saw the Blashford Lakes Natural Reserve off in the back. Earlier I'd read how former gravel pits had been turned into lakes, woods, and grassland. I'd've loved to come back in the daytime to do some serious birdwatching, but I was leaving soon.

I stood in the pub, looking round and feeling awfully alone as I scanned the room for gangsters to chat up. Not exactly what I'd planned for my holiday. Then I saw Thomas and decided to get started with him.

"Well, if it ain't old septic tank!" I turned round to see who he was talking to, and Thomas let out a roar. "Don't mind me, Abit. That's just slang for Yank." The Brits sure could put a lot of fire into that word, even when they claimed to be joking.

Thomas was dressed the same as when I first met him. Rumpled flak jacket, baggy old trousers, a wide-brimmed hat hanging down his back from a leather strap round his neck. I saw his pint glass was nearabout empty. "Whatcha drinking, Thomas? I'm getting an Old Speckled Hen." He held up his pointing finger, so I ordered two. When I brought over both pints, he was busy rolling a cigarette with a practiced, swift motion. Paper flat, tobacco sprinkled, rolled, tightened, rolled a bit more, sealed with a swipe of the tongue and a gentle, almost loving stroke. I'd seen it a million times back home.

The man next to him leaned over and asked, "How 'bout one of those rollies?" Thomas handed it to him and started the whole process again.

While he worked, he said, "People don't think I notice things, but I do."

"What have you noticed that no one thinks you have?"

"That you talk with Ian a lot." He lit up, and something in the rollie made my nose twitch. I rubbed it hard, trying not to sneeze.

"Well, people tend to do that when they don't know anyone, don't they? They cling to the ones they do know."

"Oh, that part's fine. It's just that Toby and Stanley are the ones you need to watch out for."

"That right? Why's that?"

"They asked ..." Thomas suddenly turned his back to me.

"Abit, what brings you back?"

That would be Stanley. I didn't see him walk up, but Thomas sure did. I got one of those shivers that come over me sometimes. I hadn't liked him the night before—and that evening even less.

"Because he's playing the mando tonight." Roy Arthur Lewis said, his arm extended with a beautiful mando in hand.

"For me?" I asked, happy he'd stopped by in the nick of time.

"And to calm you down," he whispered, a fake smile plastered on his face as he leaned in close to mine. "What's gotten into you? Your face is all red and you look ready to pop." Then he said for everyone to hear, "I thought this might be just the ticket."

"When do we play?"

"Not for a while. I'll let you know." Under his breath he added, "Get a grip. And you'll find Ian in the back garden."

I nodded my goodbyes to Thomas and Stanley and took my pint outside. Ian was leaning on a brick pillar, looking out at the lake.

"What lake is that?" I asked.

"Oh, hello, Abit. It's Rockford Lake. Cracking fine sight, isn't? I'd rather be out there fishing or birdwatching."

"Not five minutes ago I said the same thing myself!"

"Well, you're on vacation. Why aren't you doing that?"

I wished I'd thought before I spoke. Bringing something like that up was just asking for trouble. I scrambled to cover my mistake. "Oh, I did get to do some of that today, but tonight I wanted to play the mando. I need to feel the notes under my fingers again."

"Did Lewis bring you a mando like he promised?"

I couldn't remember Roy Arthur saying that in front of Ian, but I played along. I held up the mando and took a closer look at it myself. It was a sweet little thing with a spruce top that looked kinda like an A model, but with a wider teardrop shape. I gave it a strum, and I could hear it was bright and jangly enough to get up and dance a jig—not all dark and woody like my bluegrass F5 back home.

After that, we just stood there, both of us lost about what to say next. Finally, Ian spoke. "So how do you know Steady Hand Steadman?"

I was so surprised he'd mentioned Nigel that I just kinda stared at him. Then I chimed in with "Who?" Not the cleverest comeback, but as it turned out, the right one. I'm pretty sure my bewilderment came off as if I really didn't know who he was talking about.

"Nigel Steadman?" he asked. But before the name was fully outta his mouth again, he turned sorta pale, like he'd just thought of something awful. "Oh, never mind. I got my wires crossed."

I wasn't sure what all that was about, so I moved on. "I talked a lot about myself last night, Ian. Didn't give you a chance to say much, and we got interrupted when you were going to tell me what you do for a living."

"Oh, this and that. I'm not sure anymore. I'm thinking of shoving off from here."

"What does that mean?"

"Do something different. Make a change."

"A change from what?" I tried for a chuckle, but it died when he glared at me.

"Like I said, a change from *this and that*. I didn't inherit my old man's wealth like you did."

What could I say? I'd set that up. "Well, I've always found change a good thing. I hope you come across something you enjoy doing from day to day—or night to night, as the case may be."

"What's that supposed to mean?"

"Easy, Ian. Nothing untoward. I have to work a lot of nights at the grocery, that's all I meant." I looked down at his empty pint. "Can I get you anothern?"

"I like the way you say that. *Anothern*. And yeah, why not?"

I felt hot and sweaty by the time I got to the bar. Roy Arthur saw me, but he knew better than to come over. He just shouted, "Ten minutes," and I couldn't wait to get up on that stage.

When I went back, Ian was chatting with a pretty woman. She held his arm, so maybe it was a date. Whatever, she seemed to have put him in a better mood. I handed him his Guinness, and he smiled. "Thanks, Abit. Sorry about my short fuse. Things haven't been going my way, lately. Lots of pressure at work."

"At this and that?"

He nodded, this time smiling. "I want you to meet Pippa. She's one of my co-workers. She just came to tell me we have to leave early tonight, so I'll miss your music."

Pippa smiled and added, "Oh, we can catch the first part. We don't have to be in Sopley until ten o'clock. That's when Clive is expecting us."

Ian gave her a funny look, and she shrugged. I swear I saw her mouth something about *hayseed*. Well, we'd see about that.

"Got boss problems?" I asked. "My employees are always nagging me about being hard on them, but you've got to see it from both sides.

I try to keep the business running at the same time I take care of them."

"Nobody's ever taken care of me," Ian said. "But that's a story for another day. I see Lewis motioning for you. Break a leg, I think they say, or is that only for theater? We'll be leaving soon, but I'll see you tomorrow night?"

I just nodded. I was hoping I'd be back in Dublin by then. I said my goodbyes and headed for the loo. I needed to text Nigel. He was parked well outside the pub, waiting for a signal that Ian was leaving. That done, I hopped up on stage.

Earlier that evening, I'd showed the band the chord progressions of some of my favorite tunes. They weren't all that familiar with bluegrass, but they followed along just fine. And I made that old mando sing, if I do say so myself. We played sprightly tunes like "Soldier's Joy" and "Jenny Lynn." I wanted people to go home feeling good after an evening of music and fellowship. Thomas caught my eye as he kept time with both feet (he was sitting on a barstool) and even Stanley was toe-tapping.

Just as we were finishing "Jenny Lynn," I noticed Ian was still round, talking in the back to some guy I didn't recognize. I hoped Marcia could catch his name. (She was studying them from behind a post.) Ian and Pippa turned and followed him outside. I knew I had to get word to Nigel. I mouthed my apologies to Roy Arthur and the rest of the band and scooted out to where Nigel was parked. He'd kept the motor running after that last crank job.

I slipped into the passenger seat, getting it right that time. "Did you get my text?" I asked.

"Yeah, and I've been waiting donkey's years."

"I know. Ian and someone named Pippa left and came back. But now they're walking over yonder toward where they musta parked."

"Oh, so Pippa's joined the gang, has she?"

"Who is she?"

"Just someone I used to work with." He got a wistful look that had more than a tinge of sadness.

"That reminds me. Ian asked me how I knew you, Steady Hand Steadman."

"What? We've been so careful. How could he know anything about you and me?" He thought a while and added, "There's a mole somewhere. I just feel it." He turned back to the steering wheel, changed gears, and added, "Let's see where that slippery fellow is going tonight."

Chapter 19
Abit

BEFORE I COULD GET outta the car, Nigel pulled away from his hiding spot with his lights off. It stayed light here longer than back home, especially given it was
almost the longest day of the year, but the heavy clouds worked in our favor, making it dark enough that normally a person would need headlights.

We idled a while, waiting for Ian to appear—and yes, I could've gotten out at that point, but I flashed on the thrill of tailing the con artist we called Big Mama back in Virginia and decided to stay. It was better than lurking in a pub with another pint I didn't really want. Nigel spotted Ian and Pippa as they pulled outta the carpark, and he carefully moved forward and followed them.

We travelled along winding lanes for several miles before they turned into a driveway that led to a stone house that sent a rush of fear through me. It was more exposed, and I just knew someone would spot us. Nigel pulled into a place where trees stood between us and the house. "Now listen, lad, even I have some scruples," he said. "I don't want you sneaking up on them. We can learn a lot just by watching."

I agreed. Besides, the leaden sky had opened, letting loose a cold drizzle. While we sat there, keeping watch, I told Nigel about Big Mama and how Della and I cased her and her so-called kids. As I spun the tale, I felt a surge of energy shoot through me. Funny how life has a way of doubling back on itself, like that first time was a rehearsal for something even more important. Those ponies too. Seeing them again made me feel like I was ready for whatever lay ahead.

I sat there a while, squirming in part because of the small car, but mostly because I was itching to do something. Finally, I grabbed the car door handle and opened it as quiet as I could. No light came on—the old car's interior lights had given up the ghost long ago. Nigel tried to stop me, his face creased with worry.

"We can't see what they're doing on the backside, Nigel. I'll just have a look round back, hugging those trees."

"Be careful, Abit. And, uh, thanks." It was a small gesture, but sometimes that's all it takes to feel better about someone.

I crept round the stand of trees and came up level with the back of the house. The trees ended abruptly, like someone had done a bunch of bad bulldozer work. I peered round the little cover they gave me. I could see four or five guys busy carrying all kinds of loot. One stood guard, but he was looking toward the road. It appeared they were clearing out the house, including couches, beds, chairs, and a dining table. Then came ten, maybe more, flat-screen TVs and a few stereos. I didn't see any jewelry, but I remembered helping folks move their homes, and we always started with the biggest stuff. Maybe the jewelry was yet to come.

I inched closer to windows on my side of the house, away from the guard and all the activity. My foot caught on a root, and I stumbled, letting out a noisy "oof." Lucky for me I was behind the house by then; I didn't think anyone saw or heard me.

I was hoping to catch them filling boxes with pearls and jewelry and other treasure, but of course that would've been too easy. When I looked inside, I didn't see much. I waited a while, trying to see or hear Ian or Pippa, but they musta been in another part of the house. Just as I was easing away from the window, two guys I'd never seen before came into the room. Oddly, they were both dressed in suits and ties, looking very dapper. The taller guy kept backing up, and I nearly fell offa the stump I was standing on when I saw why. The shorter one was pointing a handgun at his middle. I looked over both shoulders to make sure he didn't have a sidekick doing the same to me.

I knew that in England having a gun wasn't like back home. People didn't have guns near as much as we did, though I figured gangsters knew how to get them. But what really caught my eye was the gunslinger had only one arm, his left suitcoat sleeve pinned up near the armhole.

When I was about to run back to the car, the one-armed guy put his gun away behind his back, tucked in his waistband like they do on TV, and the two of them stood nose to nose and spat words at each other. Then the gunslinger stormed outside. I could smell tobacco smoke, and I figured he musta lit up. I heard another voice—maybe Ian's—walking close to the corner of the house where I was standing. I pressed against the stone exterior and eased into a covered set of stairs that led to some kind of a cellar. It offered me cover, but I knew I needed to get outta there.

Before I could move, the wind shifted, and the stinky smoke from what I now recognized as a British rollie wafted over me. I held my nose shut between my thumb and pointing finger and willed myself not to sneeze. I thought about Mollie and the boys and Fiona, not necessarily in that order. I breathed slow through my mouth and let go of my nose gradual-like. I thought I was over it, but then it gave another twitch.

I nearly crawled back to the tree line and then eased over to the car. I slipped in and closed the door before I sneezed real big. Nigel jumped, but I doubted anyone could hear over all the commotion they were making.

"Boyo, you nearly made me heart seize up," Nigel said. "I could just make you out in the shadows. What happened?"

"I didn't see anything small getting packed up. Seemed to be a lot of furniture and mostly TVs and stereos. But when I looked in the window, some guy was up in some other guy's face, and he had a gun."

"Good lord, Abit. I never intended things to get this rough. Let's head back to the Dog & Bone and see if you can't get information in a more civilized fashion."

"Oh, yeah, and the guy with the gun—he only had one arm. He seemed to know his way round that gun, though, and ..."

"What did you just say?"

"What, about the gun?"

"No, the guy holding it."

"He had one arm. His suitcoat sleeve was ..."

"I know, I know. Pinned just below the armhole."

"How did you know?"

"He's Nigella's husband, Miles."

Chapter 20
Abit

"Abit, we're ready for another set. You in?"

Roy Arthur was looking at me kinda funny. Nigel had just dropped me off at the Dog & Bone, and I was still shaken by the news about Nigella's husband. I didn't really know what to make of it, but I knew I needed to forget all that and play more of that beautiful mando he'd brought for me. Somehow I managed to sound pretty decent. When Roy Arthur asked me to play "Wheel Hoss," one of my favorites, I lost myself—and my jangled nerves—in a long mando break. We played a few more and closed up for the evening.

With Ian and the rest of the gang gone, I didn't have to worry about playing detective anymore that evening. Roy Arthur had some things to tidy up, so I walked out back to enjoy the view of the lakes. Something about being near water soothes the soul. As I looked out over the water, I felt a sense of relief come over me. It was time to go home, by way of Dublin.

Roy Arthur acted real kind on the drive back to the Bridgewater Arms. "I thought you were a pretty good fiddle player," he said, "but the mando is most assuredly your instrument. I hope we can play again sometime." He lifted his topless boater slightly in a gentlemanly way of paying his respects.

Back at my hotel, Cilla came over and whispered (closer to my ear than was really necessary or proper) that Nigel was expecting me in the backroom. Everyone was sitting round the table again, waiting on me and Roy Arthur.

I was tired and eager to go upstairs and pack, so I got right down to business. "Nigel, did you talk with Miles Whatever-his-name-is? Did you find out what he was doing with that gun?

"We're working on that, Abit."

"How? When?"

"Well, I'm trying to get an appointment at the jail to see Nigella so we can straighten that out, but no one is calling me back. I tried Miles first, but he won't answer. Something's off. I swear it's a mole."

After everyone looked suspiciously at each other, we moved on to comparing notes. They were more excited about what we'd accomplished that evening than I'd expected. "You're a clever clogs, Abit," Marcia told me, though I didn't feel that way. I hadn't gotten much outta Ian.

Marcia, on the other hand, had. She'd watched while I talked with them, and when I went to buy a round, she caught a conversation between Ian and Pippa and that other bloke, who she called Daryl. Seemed Daryl was well-known for pinching—and fencing—fine jewelry. She could see him saying they were taking "everything to Langford tomorrow after it got packaged up and ready to go." The club talked about whether Langford might be a town where they planned to fence the stuff, or more than likely, someone's name.

Something Marcia'd said bothered me. "They were standing out on the deck at the Dog & Bone, Marcia, and it was pretty dark by then. How could you see their lips?"

She beamed. "Oh, Nigel got me a fine pair of Night Owl night vision binoculars that must have cost a bomb. Dear Nigel, he thinks of everything."

When I choked on my lager, no one even looked my way. Yeah, Nigel thinks of everything, all right—as long as it benefits *him*. I didn't know if it was a delayed reaction to the latest house caper or me coming to my senses at long last, but I was tired of it all. Finished. Ready to see my boys.

"Okay, like I said earlier, I'm done here," I said to no one and everyone. "My family needs me back in Dublin. It's been nice meeting all of you personally, but otherwise, this has been the vacation of my dreams, as in nightmares. What is it you all say? Cheerio!"

I nearabout ran to my room.

I HAD JUST FINISHED packing my suitcase when someone knocked on my door.

"Who is it?"

"It's me, Abit dear." Marcia. They sent the sweet one.

"I'm not changing my mind," I called out through the closed door.

"Okay, dear, but just let me in for a minute."

And, of course, that was my big mistake. She talked to me about how much it would mean for me to be at the Dog & Bone just one more night, and I could play music most of the time. "I know you are ready to see the back of us, dear, but we really do need you. Then we'll be sorry to see you go, but go you must to your family. Oh, please say yes." She took my hand and held it close to her heart.

Marcia went on for a bit more, and I couldn't think of anytime someone had talked that nice to me, other than maybe Della and Fiona, on one of her better days. Then I thought of my last hope to stave off her request for more time. I asked her about her saying she'd take me to Stonehenge. I was sure she'd try to get out of that, but when she told me she had all day the next day to show me round, what could I say? I *really* wanted to see those stones, and who knew when I'd ever have another chance?

When she finally left, I texted Fiona. I said I was just checking on her and the boys. She wrote back WE'RE FINE. HAVING WONDERFUL TIME WITHOUT YOU. Then she added one of those stupid smiley faces. I told myself it was just her sense of humor.

Chapter 21
Della

WHAT A BUZZKILL TO finish each day looking at videos from the store. Not only was it boring, but the overriding negativity of my vigil was taking its toll. So I started running through some footage at fast speed when people like Alex, Cleva, or Myrtle Ledford were in the frames. (Myrtle was an old friend who'd give back a penny if she found one out in the parking lot.) It made me miss Abit too. It didn't seem right that he wasn't in any of the videos. He was a bright spot at Coburn's.

But other than looking for a crook (or crooks!) day in and day out, things were rolling along pretty well in Laurel Falls. Annie was taking on more and more duties. Rascal had a new friend who came to play once a week while his owner/companion shopped. And I found a vendor who made enough dilly beans, apple chutney, and onion marmalade to sell me a case or two each month. Assuming we could catch Coburn's thief, things were looking up.

Chapter 22
Abit

I HEARD A CAR HORN toot while I was talking with Cilla in the Bridgewater Arms lobby. I was glad to see it was Marcia, because I'd been looking for a way of getting outta there without being rude. Let's just say Cilla was the friendly type.

I felt relieved to finally get to do something special—with someone besides myself. Marcia assured me she loved going to Stonehenge; apparently she's like a local tour guide for her guests and family.

The prehistoric monuments are about nine miles north of Salisbury, so we passed the cathedral again on the way to the village of Amesbury. According to Marcia, Amesbury is considered the oldest occupied settlement in Great Britain, founded round 8820 B.C. Man, that's old.

Apparently it's not easy to get tickets, especially in the summer, but Marcia winked at me and told me she had her ways. Just one more thing I didn't want to know more about. (I wouldn't normally think such dark thoughts, but she was a friend of Nigel's, after all.) She refused to let me repay her, but she did accept my offer to buy our lunch afterwards.

As we rode deeper into the countryside, a giant patchwork of farmland opened up before us, squares of brown and gold and green stopping and starting in a colorful pattern I'd like to try in marquetry when I got home. As I scanned the fields, I saw the stone monuments rise on the horizon, making the hair on the back of my neck stand up. I'd studied Stonehenge in books, but I never expected to get to see it. The history and mystery of those giant stones overwhelmed me. It's hard to fathom how they got them all the way from Wales, some two-hundred mile away, without trucks or technology—all the while dressed in skirts and sandals, according to the pictures in the visitor center. I just shook my head. Sometimes Shiloh and I can barely handle the trees and boards we use for our furniture (though I could imagine Shiloh taking to those skirts and sandals).

By the time we stopped for lunch, I was starving. (When am I not?) I'd been eyeing fish and chips, and believe me, these were worth the wait. The real thing in Blighty, not frozen fish from a North Carolina grocery. I almost ordered anothern!

On the way home, I asked Marcia about something I'd been wondering about: other projects the club had taken on.

"Oh, a few months ago my mother fell victim to one of those phone scammers," she said. "Gave them money she needed for food, for heaven's sake. The club worked a fine fiddle, and somehow through his hacking, Graham got most of her money back." She thought a while and added, "And last year, Malcolm's daughter got picked up for shoplifting, but she swore she didn't do it. Of course, it's easy to deny such a thing, but we believed her. Turns out, after surveillance of that shop, we proved they were pulling an insurance fraud using shoplifting as the reason for their losses when really they were just doing a lousy job of running their business."

"How'd you figure that out?"

"Miles—Nigella's husband—and Graham hacked into their accounting system. And Nigel helped with a little forgery." She musta seen my face fall and patted my arm. "This time for the good, dear."

After that, Marcia filled me in on each of the club members. She laughed when I asked her if the club was her full-time job. "No, dear, I'm a sous chef most of the time. I love to cook—even just everyday things like shepherd's pie and spaghetti Bolognese—oh, and I make a mean full English."

I recalled Roy Arthur saying he was a music teacher, but not until Marcia explained more about that did I learn he traveled round the schools and worked with kids. I chuckled when I thought about him wearing that hat inside a school like I went to. I asked Marcia if they made him take it off.

She gave me a weak smile. "People think that hat is an affectation, Abit, but he has terrible scars on his scalp from a house fire that killed his wife and little girl. He cuts the top to keep it from irritating his head." She sighed. "We don't always know what makes people tick, do we?" She paused, knowing I felt bad about my earlier comment, but after a few moments added, "You'll be glad to know that Graham really is an astonishingly good computer geek, and Nigel, well you know Nigel."

When I asked about her family, she said she'd been divorced for decades. "Did you ever want to remarry?"

"*Want* yes, but that's the easy part, isn't it? I've had no luck with the *who.*"

Even though I kept sticking my foot in it, we really did have a grand time.

THE EVENING—MY LAST IN Blighty, and I meant it this time!—we, as in the club I couldn't wait to stop being a member of, met to go over everything we'd learned in the past few days.

First, Graham and Alfred reported that none of their other leads panned out. That put our full focus on Ownbey's gang, which had two cottages jammed with stolen stuff. Marcia and her Owl binoculars learned that, thanks to

Daryl's big mouth with easy-to-read rubbery lips, smaller treasures were headed for the fence guy or the town named Langford. Together, it all sounded like we'd come up with a lot, but after a few attaboys, we knew what we had wasn't enough to get Nigella off.

We all agreed that I should come right out and ask Ian if he'd like to lead a different life, just to see how he felt about flipping to our side. So far he'd only claimed he was fed up with his life, but he didn't seem to be doing much to get out of it.

AT THE DOG & BONE, I was beginning to recognize people, especially since quite a few men seemed to live there. I hadn't realized how regular-like men went to the pub— drinking, betting on everything under the sun, and telling each other tales. While I sipped my pint of Boddington's, I overheard an overweight, grizzled guy complaining about the "old lady" expecting him home early to help with the kiddies because he'd been at the pub every night "since forever." He ground his thumb into his palm, like she had him under her thumb. Everyone nearby laughed, except me.

As I finished the last of my pint, I saw Roy Arthur setting up the music stage. I felt my spirits lift. Until I heard someone call my name.

"Abit, you're becoming a regular." Ian, of course, looking right smart in a red sweater. We were standing near the stage, and I knew we were in Roy Arthur's way, so I stepped toward a corner of the pub. Ian followed me. "I'm curious why you keep coming here. I mean the pub at the Bridgewater Arms in Lyndhurst is nicer than this one."

Again I had this funny feeling I'd never mentioned where I was staying, but I'd talked to so many people, I couldn't say for sure. "Oh, it's the music. And Roy Arthur Lewis has been so nice to me, what with me not knowing anyone. Other than my aunt."

"Oh, that's right. How's she doing? National Health isn't perfect, but I believe it's better than the care you get in the States."

"You're right about that." I'd agree with just about anything he had to say to get past this charade about Auntie Bradshaw, though something about his tone told me he saw right through my story. "And, er, it's my last night to play music—then I'm off to Dublin to join my family."

"I hope you've had a good trip—not too much time spent looking for answers you'll never find."

What in the world did that mean? "And you," I said after a beat, "I hope you can spend time finding a way of life that suits you better."

We were sparring with verbal swords, but I was feeling way outta my league. Ian smiled, then nodded. "How would you know about that, boyo?"

"You've mentioned it every night I've been here. That you were looking for a change. *Shoving off from here* I believe were your exact words."

"Ah, yes. That would be the drink talking. And there is change, and then there is change."

We were just talking nonsense. I wanted to get away from all that banter, but the rains had come back, lashing against the pub's exterior and stranding me. "That sounds like riddles talking," I said. "Life's too short not to do what you want."

Ian was quiet for a moment, like he was about to confide in me. But then Toby came by and whispered something in his ear before moving on. The moment was lost. That was when I decided to go for broke. "Before I go back to Dublin, Ian, I want to come clean with you. You know earlier, when I told you I owned a chain of grocery stores and a big farm, I was just blowing smoke. On a lark. In truth, I'm an ordinary woodworker and musician. I live on a nine-acre farm, which is next to nothing back home. My father did run a grocery store—right into the ground."

Ian stared at me for what felt like an hour or two, then burst out laughing. "And here I thought you were a grocery magnate."

I looked round for something to hold, something to do with my hands. I suggested I buy us a round.

"No, my shout, Abit. What'll you have? And yes, let's talk about next chapters in our lives. I'll be right back."

Only he wasn't. He musta gotten waylaid. Roy Arthur called me up to the stage, where one last time I launched into a few Bill Monroe favorites like "East Tennessee Blues" and "Bluegrass Stomp."

When our set was over, I did see Ian again, but he seemed different. Nervous-like. As I walked his way, he just waved and mouthed "Sorry" before turning and going out the door. Not *goodbye*, not *good to meet you*. That struck me as odd, so I followed him.

I eased out the front door and walked quiet-like till I heard some chatter. I peeked round a corner, into a dark space, cobblestones shiny from the evening's rain. Ian was talking to a copper Nigel had pointed out earlier. Someone to watch out for (of course that was what Nigel would say). I tiptoed back to the pub and texted Nigel what I'd just seen. He was likely idling nearby and would want to see this for himself. The other stuff Ian said could wait till our recap meeting later that evening.

When I got back to the bar, Stanley and Reggie were standing there. They motioned me over to their end and asked if they could buy me a pint. "One for the road to Dublin?" Stanley asked.

"Hey, thanks, that's nice of you." I didn't really want it, but it seemed like a kind gesture not to be sneezed at on this awful trip. I took a sip of the frothy Guinness, and the bitter brew went down my parched throat just fine.

After a few more sips, I shook their hands and said my goodbyes. To be honest, *good riddance* was on the tip of my tongue.

And that was the last thing I remembered.

Part Two
Down Under

Chapter 23

Abit

"Go on, just let your mouth hang open. It feels better that way, even if it makes you look barmy."

My head was pounding, eyes blurry, but I could've sworn a kid was sitting on a chair next to the bed I was lying on, talking to me.

"Conor?" I asked.

"Not me, matey."

I musta fallen back to sleep because when I woke, whoever I'd talked to earlier had gone. I rubbed my eyes to see better, but I was still in a strange room. Then I rubbed my head, the way you do when you're confused. "Ow!"

"Yeah, you took a tumble at the pub. It's just a small bump."

He was back, standing over me. Kinda stocky, but more like strong than fat. He'd grow up to be a big guy, so I was grateful he was still a young'un.

But it was more than a bump that made my head ache. My brain felt like it was floating in molasses, and though I couldn't remember ever being drugged before, I knew that had to be it. I had a foggy recollection that I'd waked up earlier in the pitch black on a sorry old bed and thought I was dead. Crazy, middle-of-the-night thoughts? As I looked round the windowless room, I wasn't sure.

"Where am I? I've got to get home to my family. I've got two boys about your age, and I'm missing them something fierce."

"You talk funny."

That again. I was sick and tired of it—and everything going wrong. I told him so and cursed at him while I was at it.

"Hey, me and my old man don't hold with that kind of talk."

"Oh, yeah? Well I don't hold with being in a, a ..." I was having trouble finding my words. "... stinking cellar ... with a splitting headache and a stomachache."

"Sorry about that. You've probably just got the collywobbles. I don't know exactly what happened. My old man said you fainted, and he brought you here to get over it."

"Get over it? Why didn't he contact my friend, Nigel?" Then I remembered I wasn't supposed to know Nigel. All this was surely the doings of the Ownbey gang, so I figured I'd better keep up the ruse. "Or take me to the hospital?"

"He said you didn't know anyone. You're a tourist, yeah? He couldn't figure out what else to do with you. He didn't know where you were staying, and since your condition wasn't that serious, well ..." He motioned round the sorry room like it were a palace.

To move past my slip up about Nigel, I nodded in agreement, but that made my head pound like a piston. I could only hope he wouldn't tell his "old man" what I'd said. "Okay, fine, but why a dungeon? And what are you doing down here? Surely not babysitting me."

"Oh, no, I'm hiding from my mother. In the room just next door. And it's *not* a dungeon," he said as he walked over to the door. "Well, I just wanted to get you settled and check on you, what with the concussion and all. I need to excuse myself now."

Any other time I woulda laughed at him acting so proper-like, but I was starting to panic when he unlocked the door separating the two rooms and quickly relocked it on his side. I could see him through a crude partition that looked like they'd started to divide the cellar into two rooms but stopped halfway up. From there, a row of vertical two-by-fours went to the ceiling. They were spaced less than a foot apart, and I wondered why anyone would waste their money on all those extra studs just to support wallboard. Then it hit me. It was a homemade jail. I knew Ownbey was behind it now.

I noticed the heavy door had an impressive lock on it and a big slot cut in the middle of it—like I'd seen in prison movies. At least they planned to feed me, assuming the food was safe to eat.

I could see the kid walking toward what I made out to be a small kitchen on his side. "Would you like a cuppa?" he called over his shoulder, like it was the most normal thing in the world.

My room had been painted a soft yellow and the bed had a handmade coverlet, like they were making an effort to brighten things up. But they'd failed. It was dreary. The space contained just the bed, one table, and two chairs, and the opposite end had been partitioned off with cheap paneling. I hoped it was a bathroom.

I recalled seeing the grave of Alice Pleasance Liddell and thought maybe this was just a bad dream, you know, through the looking glass or down the rabbit hole. I blinked and pinched myself. I was still in a cellar.

My head was spinning, but I needed to talk reason with that boy. I got up slowly and made my way over to the jail wall between our rooms. "Okay, let's try this again. I know your old man has to be part of the Clive Ownbey gang." He gave me a funny look, so I knew there was some kind of connection, but he wouldn't budge. Just stood there waiting for me to say something else. "Okay," I said. "let's start with you. Who are *you*? "

"Well, I could ask the same of you."

"I asked first ..." I stopped and let out a long sigh. I couldn't believe I was arguing like a 10-year-old—with a 10-year-old. And I could tell from the way he crossed his arms he knew

I knew how pointless my holding out was. "All right, I'm Abit Bradshaw from Laurel Falls, North Carolina, and I have a wife and two boys waiting for me over in Dublin. And yes, I'd like a cuppa, assuming you don't poison it."

He looked over his shoulder with a world of hurt before turning on the kettle.

"Hey," I barked at him. "I told you who I am, now who are you? Like I asked the first time."

He just ignored me as he fumbled round with the tea stuff. While he was pouring water into the pot, he said, "And I don't know any Clive Ownbey," with a special emphasis on Clive. I rolled my eyes and didn't say another word till he stood at the door slot, holding a cup of tea. I reached in and brought a rather nice ivy-patterned cup and saucer over to my side.

"Come on," I said after a big gulp of tea. (Too sweet, just the way Vern likes his, but I still welcomed it.) "I told you my name. What's yours?"

"Baldy."

I looked at his full head of hair. "Strange name."

He just shrugged, running his hand through his blonde mop. "My dad's bald, so I figure I'll live into it. What did you say your name is?"

"Abit."

"And you made fun of *my* name?"

Rather than argue, which only made my head hurt worse, I told him how I came upon that name. He made a face when I explained how people back home poked fun at me for being "a bit slow." I wasn't going for pity, but if my tale of woe helped loosen this kid up, I'd use it.

He looked kinda sad when he next spoke. "My parents named me Archibald, or I should say my mother did. That was the name of some relative of hers, and she forced my old man to agree to drop it on me. I hated it—and all the teasing I got for it at school. So when I changed it to Baldy, that helped. Maybe you should change yours."

"I tried that. Della, a friend of mine, said I should go by my initials, but VJ never stuck."

"What did that stand for?"

"Vester Junior."

"You've got to be kidding me. You really got a raw deal in the name department." He rubbed his chin in an impressive imitation of an old man. "You're a Yank. Maybe I'll just call you Yank, short for bloody Yank!"

"Fine. Whatever." I'd heard that so many times in the past week, I didn't care anymore. Really, I thought the Brits were more clever than this.

I started feeling woozy, so I laid on the bed again. Next thing I knew Baldy was talking to someone coming down the steps, over by the door where I couldn't see anything. I got up careful-like and headed that way, but by then the kid was saying, "Ta" and putting the tray on the small table in the kitchen. I did get a glimpse of someone's hands—more like a man's than a woman's. That was as far as my detecting went.

In a little while, Baldy said breakfast was ready. I stood up but felt kinda dizzy, so I sat back down on the bed. When I stayed there a while, he called out, "Don't let it get cold," like my 50-year-old mother used to do. I shuffled over to the door and took the tray from him. I had to say it was a fine spread.

He had the same food on his plate, so I watched him start scarfing it down. "Whatcha looking at?" he asked with his mouth full. "Your food's *not* poisoned, if that's what you're thinking. You better eat up, Yank. It's your last chance for hours."

"You know, for someone who acts all high and mighty about not swearing, you've got quite a mouth on you. And where did you hear that term *bloody Yank* if you and your old man don't hold with such talk?"

"On the telly." As if that explained everything.

"Well, real life is a good bit different from the telly." I paused, thinking back on what I'd just said. "Though being stolen and hidden in a cellar by some crazy man and his sidekick kid sounds like a show I might've seen before."

"Keep talking to me like that and things could get a lot worse." He'd gotten up and walked over to the jail wall, where I could see him striking a large spoon in the palm of his other hand. He may have been close to Conor and Vern's ages, but he seemed a lot older. And bigger. His words scared me.

I HAD TO ADMIT the breakfast was better than many I'd made. I reckoned you'd call it a half-English with eggs over easy, rashers, tomatoes, mushrooms, and toast and marmalade. And tea. Oncet I sat down, I ate like I hadn't eaten in forever. To be honest, I couldn't remember my last meal. The tea was hot and strong, the eggs and mushrooms perfect, and the rasher one of the best I'd had. I thanked Baldy. He nodded in a practiced way that worried me. He seemed so calm, as though, somehow, he'd done all this before.

When we'd both finished, Baldy told me to bring the dishes to the slot; he picked them up and carried them to his sink. As he was washing up, he called over his shoulder, "My old man says Yanks are pillocks."

I really was getting tired of that refrain, but no point in getting riled up with this kid. "Well, we do have our share of idiots, or as you call them, eejits," I conceded. "And I know for a fact you have them here too."

Baldy turned with a "put up your dukes" look on his face. "Are you talking about me and my old man?"

"Well, no, I don't know you. But I've met eejits in lots of places round here, which I believe is somewhere near Ringwood."

"Where?"

"Where what?"

"Where did you meet these eejits, eejit?"

"Oh, right. Well, I met one in Liverpool recently. And I've been to Lyndhurst, though no sign of one there. Yet."

"You're making fun of me now."

"Maybe a little."

"Where else have you been?"

"Dublin and Clifden in Ireland and in the States, Washington, D.C.; Boone and Laurel Falls, North Carolina; and all over Virginia."

"That's a good many places. I never go anywhere."

"Not yet, but you will."

"Oh, yeah, how do you know?"

"I just do." *Like wherever they lock up juvenile delinquents.*

"That's one way of seeing things, but I think we see the world different-like." Baldy crossed his arms again and looked at me sternly.

"Oh yeah, how do you see it?"

"I think ... that ... well ... my old man and I ..."

"Don't you ever think for yourself? You can, you know. So what if you're just a kid ... you've got ideas don't you?"

"I'm too young."

"To have ideas? Who says?"

"My old man."

"Well, of course he does. That's what fathers do sometimes. I've used that lame excuse on my own boys from time to time. But step back and think about it. You are a living, breathing human being, and you have opinions and ideas. When I was your age, my daddy used to stare at me in a way that made me go all funny inside. Like nothing I could ever think up would be worth a toot. But I've learned he was wrong. Dead wrong." Baldy looked at me like I'd said the earth weren't round and snuffled, something I noticed he did often. This dank cellar wasn't good for either of us.

I went back to my bed and longed for even that old copy of "Woman's Own." I lay there for a while and finally fell back to sleep to the sounds of a 10-year-old doing the dishes.

Chapter 24
Nigel

I KNEW ABIT WAS fed up with me, so I wasn't surprised he didn't come downstairs the next morning when I had Cilla ring his room. Busy packing was my guess. More's the pity our visit had gone so poorly, though at least he saw Stonehenge and got to play some music. People were raving about his mandolin playing, so he could go home with those good feelings.

Later that afternoon, Marcia rang me. "The boy's clothes and belongings are all still in his room, Nigel, but the bed hasn't been slept in. I'm telling you, he's nowhere to be found."

"Oh, he's just gone for a walk, I'm sure. Maybe he decided to stay another night after all."

"No, the front desk woman told me he didn't show for breakfast or lunch."

"So he ate in town. He likes his early mornings out with the birds and whatever."

"Well, I hope you're right, Nigel. But I got the impression he'd had his swan song last night. Some of the others are quite concerned as well."

By that evening, I'd joined them.

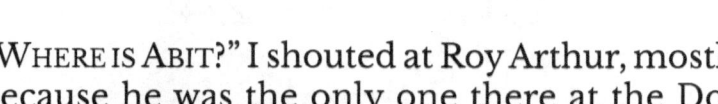

"WHERE IS ABIT?" I shouted at Roy Arthur, mostly because he was the only one there at the Dog & Bone. Getting ready for that night's music, I presumed.

"Don't look at me, Nigel. He's your ward, not mine. I just gave him rides, and he stood me up last night." He turned to walk away.

"Hold up, man. Show a little respect. He's been a big help to us. We're a lot further along now than before he arrived."

"Listen, Nigel, I know you're upset, but I honestly don't know anything."

"What do you mean he stood you up?"

"I was supposed to give him a ride back to Lyndhurst. A couple of blokes stopped me to talk about music lessons, and I kept trying to get away from them, but they were soon-to-be paying customers, yeah? I didn't think it would matter if I was a bit late. But by the time I got to the front of the pub, everyone had left except for a few staff. None of them knew anything about Abit. I hate to think about it now, but maybe those two blokes were part of Ownbey's gang, waylaying me while they did something to the boy." He started to leave, then called over his shoulder, "Look, I'm really sorry, Nigel. He's a nice kid. Check with the barman. Maybe he saw something."

I knew which one he was talking about. Big guy, ruddy complexion, though that didn't narrow it down much when it came to publicans and bartenders. I looked all round but couldn't find him. When I asked one of the staff, she said he'd be in after five o'clock. I ordered a tonic and lime and waited.

I saw him when he clocked in for his shift. He was barely behind the bar before I was all over him with questions. He started straightening his work area, obviously none too pleased with how the lunch crew had left things.

"Yeah, I saw him last night. I believe he was hanging out with that Reggie character and another guy. Just after I gave the shout, he said he was tired and called a taxi to take him wherever he was staying."

"But he had a ride."

"He told me to tell that Roy Arthur guy—the one with the funny hat—that he needed to go on."

"Did you?"

"Did I what?"

"Tell Roy Arthur."

"I tried, but I didn't see him." He shrugged. "Sorry mate. We were busy closing. He'll turn up. Men on their own in a foreign country ... you know."

"Yes, I do know. You're the one who doesn't know. Abit is a fine lad. He isn't out there *you-knowing*." I pounded my fist on the bar to punctuate my displeasure.

"Okay, okay. Just trying to help cheer you up," he said, his hands up in a surrender pose. "I'll let you know if he comes in tonight. Give me your number."

We left it at that.

I asked round a bit more, but no one recalled seeing Abit after last call. They all remembered his music playing, but after that he just vanished. The barmaid said that evening had been too busy to recall anyone in particular. With one staff person calling in sick, they were run ragged.

I went off grumbling to myself. This wouldn't've happened if I hadn't needed to act as though I didn't know Abit. Then again, it wouldn't've happened if I hadn't gotten involved with Nigella. Oh, it was a right mess. I felt sick, in part because if anything had happened to that boy, Della would kill me. And I wasn't speaking in hyperbole.

Chapter 25
Abit

WHEN I WOKE AGAIN, I didn't know if it was day or night. No windows to offer a clue, though I assumed since the lights were on, it was still daytime. And I could see Baldy was awake, sitting in a chair over by the kitchen.

I sat up and rubbed my eyes, then walked to the jail wall. "Now, listen, Baldy. That was a very nice breakfast. Thank you and whoever prepared it. But I'm ready to leave now. Could you ring upstairs or clang the pipes with that spoon you were threatening me with earlier so I can get outta your way?"

"Not just yet. Concussions are dangerous. You need to rest."

"I'm rested."

"Not enough."

I knew for certain this had nothing to do with a so-called faint. I'd been drugged, and the Ownbey gang was behind it. I also knew Nigel would realize I was missing and put the club to work finding me. At least I hoped he didn't assume I'd left for Dublin the way I'd been threatening.

I turned on my side and dozed, in and out. I really was exhausted from the entire trip. In addition to jetlag, I hadn't slept well at Quinn's house—the bed was lumpy and small, and I kept rolling over onto Fiona, which of course annoyed her. Then all those escapades with Nigel. I was give out.

Later, I got up and started looking round the room for some kind of escape route. Baldy came over to the studs to see what I was up to. He got a big smirk on his face, and I thought terrible things about what I'd like to do to him.

"You might as well settle down," he said, as though he were talking to a dog. "You need your rest." Medical advice from a child. Was there any end to the long line of people ready to tell me how to live my life?

"Well at least tell me *something* about where I am. Am I in the pub's basement? In Ringwood? London? The woods? And who's guarding me besides you? I mean if I *did* get upstairs, would someone shoot me?" I was babbling, but I was desperate for more information.

"You'll see for yourself soon enough," Baldy said as he headed over to a table and chair in the corner of his side of the room.

"It doesn't feel that way."

"You will."

He turned on a bright light that had been rigged up over his table and began working on some kind of model ship. It appeared to be a submarine, and from the swastika on the box lid, it musta been German. He kept his head down and worked for a while before calling out, "You're deep in the forest."

I lay on my bed, trying to not say anything or otherwise involve myself in this strange situation. I wasn't sure how much time had gone by when outta the blue Baldy said, "You mentioned you had boys." Snuffle.

He had me there. I couldn't *not* talk about Conor and Vern. I rolled over. "I do. Me and their mama, Fiona, have two fine boys—Conor is ten and Vern is nine."

"I bet you've done everything for them." Snuffle, snuffle.

"I could never do everything I want for those boys. There's not enough time in any given day. Besides, they need to do things for themselves. Like homework. They're already better at that than I would ever be, though I'd help them if I could. Say, where's *your* homework?"

"Summer break, you daft git."

"Oh, right. But still, there must be some books you enjoy reading, even in the summer." Honestly, I was hoping he had a stash somewhere. I was ready to read anything—the British equivalent of Nancy Drew mysteries if that was all I could get my hands on. (Baldy later told me one of his favorite books was *Gangsta Granny*. I knew he and his old man were in with Clive Ownbey when he said the book was about a little boy who thinks his grandmother is boring until he finds out she's an international jewel thief!)

"Nope. Just me models. I'm good at 'em."

"I could help with that. I like to bring home models for the boys, and sometimes they let me join in."

Baldy looked at me like I'd lost my few remaining marbles. "Why would I do that? It's mine."

"Well, yes, but it's fun to work on them together."

"Maybe for you." His turned back to his model.

I rolled over, thinking about my boys.

WHEN I HEARD SOMEONE coming down the stairs with what I assumed was our lunch, I jumped up to see who it was. But of course he or she didn't step beyond the large door to my cell. I didn't even see hands this time. But I did shout. "Get me outta here! I'm fine. No concussion. You better watch out, because when I do get outta here …" But I heard the upstairs door slam and the lock turn. Baldy looked at me, embarrassed. Not about my situation, but my lame protests, which he'd already told me were pointless.

Lunch was a ploughman's. My appetite had come back in full, and I gobbled it down. Baldy made me another good cuppa, and as I sipped it, I realized I'd never asked why he was hiding from his mother. So I did.

"My old man is trying to protect me from her." Baldy sighed real big. "He says she's bad for me." He didn't look all that convinced. In fact, he looked awful sad.

"That doesn't make it so."

Baldy glared at me, I guessed because I'd questioned his daddy's thinking. But then he seemed to be thinking about what I'd just said. Like if it were true, then maybe his mother wasn't bad for him. That was all I could figure. But I held my peace; I couldn't afford to rile him.

I stayed quiet for a while. Then outta sheer boredom, I started talking again, switching things back to my childhood. I told him about Mama and Daddy and how things were when I was growing up. About getting pulled outta school and the shame of it. I wasn't even allowed to walk past the schoolyard after that. When he asked how my parents treated me now that I was grown up, I told him they had passed.

"What? Some kind of test?"

I reckoned he didn't know that expression, so I spelled it out. "They're dead, gone to their Maker. Died on the exact same date two year apart."

He got that sad look again.

I felt sick reliving my sorry youth—and mad all over again that I was stuck in that cellar, talking about things I didn't want to remember instead of being with my family and doing the things I *wanted* to do. "Listen, Baldy. Nice chatting with you and all, but I need to talk with Clive Ownbey, and I know you know who I'm talking about."

"And I'm telling you I don't. And neither does my old man."

"How do you know till you ask him?"

"I *did* ask him. While you were sleeping." Darn it! His old man must be bringing the food down, and I kept missing him. "All I know is he brought you down here for safekeeping. He said you were in danger. That's why I'm here too. My mother got custody, but she's a drunk and an addict. She got into drugs with her latest boyfriend while I was with them, and I got scared and called my old man. The coppers were looking for me, but they'll give up after searching upstairs. You would've heard them if you hadn't been snoring so loud. They might come back again, so I have to stay down here a bit longer."

Something about his story sounded made up, rehearsed even. Maybe the old man feeding him his side of the story. I asked Baldy what his life was like with each parent alone—when they weren't in the same room battling with one another. I got suspicious when he said everything was hunky-dory with the old man, and lousy with the lunatic. And maybe it was. I told him I was sorry he had to deal with all that so early in life.

"I'm tough. I can handle it."

"Yeah, I know you're working at it, but I don't believe you should have to deal with things like that at age ten."

"I'm nine."

"You don't say. You look a lot older—and taller—than that."

He changed his stance, trying to look even tougher. It sorta worked. But that still didn't make it right what his old man was putting him through. I told him that.

Baldy smirked. "What? That's supposed to make me feel better? Coming from someone who believed people when they called him slow or stupid?"

"I didn't know different!"

"Why not? You knew you weren't. I mean I know I'm not stupid, and it's stupid to let people say you are."

I could see Baldy was getting hot under the collar. "Okay, that's how you see it. Fine. You weren't there. You don't know how things were."

"Oh, great. You're going all *poor me* on me."

"If that were true, I wouldn't be here trying to get out of this darn cellar."

"Why not?"

"Because I'd probably be stuck in N.C. living with my mother."

"I thought you said she was dead."

I sighed. "What I just said was a figure of speech."

"Well, whatever, you shouldn't have thought you were stupid."

"Good, we agree. Now don't say anything for a while."

Chapter 26
Nigel

"Hey, Nigel, what happened to that kid I was talking to? I heard he's gone missing."

I wanted to knock McCafferty off his barstool, he looked so debonaire and carefree. Gangsters could be like that. The ones who were all polite and cultured put a right chill up my spine. And then it hit me. He wasn't supposed to know I knew Abit, and yet he'd asked the boy about Steady Hand Steadman. Oh, if only that moniker were still true! My hand no longer had the dexterity it once did, so intricate forgery was out. Maybe it was time to hang it up. This latest caper really wasn't going well, either, considering the way things were playing out. I thought about all the money I'd stashed away on the FTSE, enough for a fine retirement in the Azores.

Of course, I'd said all that before. The thrill never came from the lucre but the winning, especially at something you're not supposed to have. Not that the money hurt.

I tried for cavalier and hoped I'd struck just the right note. "I heard he's done a runner," I told McCafferty as vaguely as possible. "Back to Dublin to see his family. You and your gang drove him crazy."

"Not what I heard."

"I don't know who you've been listening to, but you heard wrong." Needless to say, when the news eventually came out, that is, when we finally *found* the boy, I'd look a right fool. Though when I thought about it, I was likely to anyway. Besides, maybe he *did* go to Dublin. Unfortunately, I had no way of knowing how to reach his family in Ireland. I supposed Della might, but I wasn't quite ready to involve her. I had to hope Abit just hopped a train and got out of Dodge. At that moment, that sounded good to me too.

"Listen, I know we've had our differences in the past," McCafferty said, "but I want to help find that boy."

That was rich. Ownbey and McCafferty had likely ordered one of the gang members to pick up Abit and stash him somewhere to get us to lay off. Maybe this was their way of starting those negotiations. We'd already determined the other gang Graham and Alfred were scoping out played no part in the thefts. According to Alfred, they were more into drugs, not jewelry. But I didn't want to show my hand, so I just stayed quiet to see what McCafferty was up to.

After a while, he said, "I've been asking round about him. I got a kick out of his ways. Old-fashioned and polite. And he played a fine mandolin. So I asked that big bartender, who said a taxi pulled up to take him back to wherever he was staying. Lyndhurst, wasn't it? Bridgewater Arms?"

Somebody had been doing his homework. Then he surprised me with, "But like you said, he might've been good and sick of us. I know I am. Time for a change, if you catch my drift."

There it was again, his hinting at living a different kind of life. Well, right now I didn't care about him.

Chapter 27
Abit

THAT FIRST DAY IN THE CELLAR, I didn't have my wits about me, but by that night, I was on full alert. I had trouble getting to sleep, and even oncet I did, I woke in a cold sweat. It'd come to me that my wallet and phone were missing. I got up and searched everywhere, though there were few places to look. My pockets were empty. Nothing under the bed or in the covers. Someone—likely Baldy's old man—had taken them, and with them the pictures of my family. I didn't care about the money, but those photos meant the world to me. I felt lost without them. A bad feeling came over me, like back when I was a kid and other people controlled my life, me with no way of changing that.

I wondered why Baldy was so passive about being locked up in this dank old place. He seemed kinda content washing dishes, making tea, working on his model. Then again, I guessed it wasn't that different from when I was his age. I just sat round hemmed in by Mama and Daddy's rules, keeping outta their way, left to myself. The world they'd created was as small and dark as where we sat now. And when you're a kid, you don't realize your everyday life is strange. It's just life.

I fell back into a fitful sleep until oncet again I awoke with a jolt. Back home, I'd come to appreciate these bolts outta the blue as more than irritating wakeups. It was like my mind and body knew better and stirred up ideas while I slept. Sometimes when I woke, I had new designs for my furniture or an urgent sense that one of my boys needed me. Or even something as ordinary as I'd forgotten to confirm a gig. I lay there, my heart pounding, and waited to see what this one was about.

In time, I came to understand the message—get outta that cellar! Not just because that made sense for anyone in my situation. Something else was at play, and as sure as if I'd gotten a call from heaven above, I knew I needed to make a move.

I checked on Baldy, who was kinda snoring, so I reckoned he was deep asleep. I noticed he had a nightlight between his bed and what I assumed was a bathroom. I felt sad that a boy was made to live like this, only a small light to stave off his fears. But that speck of light helped me as I tiptoed over to a corner that had all kinds of junk piled up. When my eyes adjusted a bit more, I saw it was mostly wood and old rags, a coupla chairs, and a cardboard box. I opened the box as quiet as I could. Just a tangle of odds and ends. I sat cross-legged on the cold floor and worked through the stuff so as not to make noise. It took time, but then again, I had nothing but time. I rummaged round and felt a picture frame, some coffee mugs, and a few kitchen tools. Then my hand brushed against something thin and metal. A broke-off paring knife. It was good enough for what I needed.

I held my breath as I eased over to the door and studied its lock. I'd picked a few in my day, though mostly when I'd locked myself outta the house. And *not* while my hands were shaking because I was scared outta my wits. I tried to steady myself, working slow and careful-like. When I heard a click, I managed to tamp down a victory whoop. I looked over at Baldy, but he hadn't budged. Then I pulled on the door to my freedom.

Only it didn't move. I tried again, but all I got was the same sorry click.

I went back to bed, sliding the knife under my thin mattress. An obvious spot for Baldy to check, if he were given to searching. For now, though, I felt better knowing it was there.

Eventually, I fell back to sleep and had a dream that I had a nice breakfast with Baldy and then we took a walk in the sunshine. I shared the names of some trees and birds with him. I was pointing to a bushtit when a voice in my head shouted *Run! Run!* The hollering woke me up, but it was just Baldy clattering round in the kitchen getting breakfast ready. That dream and a heavy hangover from my nighttime sorrows made for a stranger than usual meal. Neither one of us said anything till he'd cleared the breakfast dishes.

"When will *you* get out of here?" I asked, a question that had been bothering me.

"When the authorities give up looking for me. You see, no one knows about this room."

That brought on a new wave of nausea. What had he called it earlier? Collywobbles? I felt sick with fear for me and my children, as though I were forever lost in this awful place. Fiona was a good mother, but she couldn't care for two boys on her own, not with the farm and her busy job as a nurse. And what was going to happen to me? Or for that matter, Baldy? "You mean, they'll give up on a missing kid?" I asked. "How could either of your parents let that happen?"

"Well, like I said, my mother is crazy, and my father, well, he wants me. So he won't pester them; he just wants them to go away so we can be together. He's waiting for me to become one more misper they forget about."

"A what?"

"Misper. A missing person."

"But then you can't suddenly come out and start going to school. I just don't understand how this will work."

"My old man says he's got a place for us to go to where they won't know us."

"Well, why not go there now? Why wait it out here, in this horrible place?"

"Hey, watch it. I've treated you nice, haven't I?"

I couldn't answer yes because it *was* a horrible place, and I hated being there. And while Baldy had been as kind as a 9-year-old could be, the point was I was there against my will. When I didn't answer, he added, rather belligerently, "My old man has it figured out, yeah? He wants the heat off before we make the move."

Heat off. The move. More gangster-movie talk. I nodded just to end the strange conversation.

Chapter 28
Nigel

I KEPT WAITING FOR a phone call from Della giving me lip about Abit's disappearance. Nothing yet. Apparently she didn't know, which gave me time to solve this mess before her fury reached across the pond.

I'd already tried going through McCafferty. It was time to find the big man himself, Clive Ownbey. I started with Toby, but he just shook his head. No way was he setting up a meeting. "Trust me mate, that's not a good idea," he said after accepting the Guinness I'd bought him at the Dog & Bone.

I called up Marcia, but she wasn't having it either. "Oh, no. Sorry, luv. I'm gutted about that dear boy's disappearance, but no. I can't get involved with Ownbey." She sounded truly scared, and I hung up.

Ownbey was a nasty sod, no question about it. Not someone I was looking forward to meeting face to face. That night, in a last ditch effort, I put the question to Graham. He suggested an email. Said we could send it straight to Ownbey. Apparently finding the entire gang's email addresses was a "piece of cake." Amazing to me, still living in the twentieth century, that a few keystrokes delivered Ownbey's address. Graham helped me compose the note. Brief and to the point.

Ownbey, I know you're hiding my friend, Abit Bradshaw. I have information on you that I won't go to the Met with if you let him go. This is in everyone's best interest. Nigel Steadman

Even more amazing was the speed with which we got an answer:

Steadman, as usual you are full of it.

The cad didn't even sign it. (Graham explained there was no need for salutations and closings with email. Really? What was civilization coming to?) Ownbey's cryptic note left us wondering if he was merely turning down my offer or disputing that he had the boy. We were back to the beginning. And what do you do then? Well, obviously, begin again.

THE CLUB MET THAT evening at the Bridgewater Arms, away from Ownbey's territory. We went round to share everything we'd found out about Abit. Unfortunately, it didn't take long. Roy Arthur had been tapping into his music connections, and no one had heard a thing. I told them about talking with McCafferty, who'd proven useless.

"After I met with you, luv, I did contact Ian," Marcia added. "I really do want to help find Abit, so I used my old charms on him. Well, I'm afraid they are old charms, indeed, because they didn't work. Or he really doesn't know anything."

"Well, thanks for trying," I said, mopping my brow with my handkerchief. This was not going well.

"Hold on. Hold on. I'm not finished," she admonished. "I was over at the Dog & Bone when I asked Ian, and I remembered to take my Owls with me. Nigel, I can't thank you enough for purchasing those. I sneaked out to the carpark where Ian had been heading, and thanks to the field glasses I was able to get a good look at the man he was talking to—and I'm sure he's a copper."

There was a rumble of murmurs as we all commented on her discovery. I had an idea about who the copper was, and I promised to check into that. But after a bit of excitement, Graham stated the obvious: "How does any of this help us find the lad?"

Chapter 29
Abit

IT FELT LIKE A HOPELESS ambition to think I'd ever get outta there, but I hung onto it anyways. Even when the walls started to close in on me. (I kept seeing them as damp with mold growing up and down them, but really, that was all in my head.)

I reckoned being kept away from nature was messing with me. Without its abiding presence, I felt diminished, like an arm or leg had been cut off. I used to walk round the farm every day and listen to the birds. Their songs kept my spirits high. And I'd watch the chickens strut outta the barn and all through the garden, so regular-like you could set your watch by them. Here the only sounds were Baldy's snuffling and gobbly sounds from his awful table manners, which were only slightly muffled by the open wall.

And I missed my music. Earlier I'd tried singing some songs, but only the lonesome ones came to me, like "Wayfaring Stranger" or prison songs like "Shackles and Chains." After a while, Baldy hollered over for me to shut up. I know I sounded good, so he was just doing that thing people do—even kids—when they get a little power.

No one was more surprised than me when late one afternoon—was it the second or third day?—I just started to cry. I thought I'd been dealing pretty good with everything, but I sat on the edge of my bed and wept for my boys and Fiona and Mollie and my beautiful farm. I prayed to Jesus they'd be spared this craziness, and that I'd be returned to them. I thought about how the counselors at The Hicks had helped me work through the bad stuff from when I was a young'un. But they'd also warned me it was like peeling an onion—more layers to come. Well, they'd come.

I saw Baldy look up from his model, studying me with a furrowed brow. He left his model and walked to the door. I could hear him unlocking it, then relocking and coming over to me. He started patting my back. "Come on now, Abit. It's time for lunch. We've got a jolly good shepherd's pie today."

That made me cry harder. Being soothed by a boy who, though he may not yet know it, needed soothing too. Which made me recall how Conor sometimes tried to console me when things weren't going right, telling me how much he loved me, and now that made me cry all the more. After a while, I got the hiccups.

Baldy made some funny sounds, what passed for mirth from this serious child. Pretty soon I was chuckling too. I finally got it together and went over to the table and sat. Baldy went next door (unlocking and locking each time—even with food to carry) and came back with two plates under a shepherd's pie with perfectly browned potatoes on top, just like Fiona made back home. I was surprised when he set both plates down on my table and pulled up a chair. We were eating together for the first—and as it played out, only—time.

When we'd finished, Baldy reached over to pick up my plate, and I grabbed his wrist. "You know, Baldy, I'm not here because I fainted. I've only fainted oncet in my life, and that was when I saved a woman's life from a serial killer. I didn't even faint when I rescued my boys from that very same killer, so don't look like you don't know what I'm talking about."

Baldy shook his arm free. He hurried back over to his side, as much as you could hurry with all that locking up. I followed him over to the wall and called out, "Tell me what you know about Clive Ownbey. Please. I know he's the key to this. He stole a bunch of jewelry along with other things like televisions and stereos."

That was when Baldy told me I sounded like a children's book, saying it was a story right outta *Gangsta Granny*. He never exactly said he didn't know Clive Ownbey, though his blank expression when I mentioned Ian McCafferty made me think he didn't know them. But I knew his old man did.

"Listen here," I told him, "I don't know about Clive Ownbey or Ian McCafferty. Tell your old man I can't say anything that might hurt them with the law. I had some beers with Ian. Big deal. I know nothing more than Ian likes Old Speckled Hen and sometimes Guinness."

"Can't you get it through you thick head? I don't know what you're talking about." Baldy turned on a lamp before settling in for another session with his model. This time a different ship. From the picture on the box, it appeared to be one of those handsome tall ships with all the puffy sails. I guessed he'd finished the first one while I slept. That was the way in this cellar—time just vanished, drifting away, taking my life with it.

"Of course not. Just play dumb. That must come easy." Oh yeah, I'd started slinging arrows like that, and why not? I hadn't made much headway talking nice. But nothing seemed to faze him; he just kept working on his ship. "This is all some big misunderstanding," I went on, explaining how Nigel's girlfriend was innocent. As I was talking, Baldy shook his head and mumbled something about this never having happened before. I couldn't figure what that meant. I just chalked it up to the whole awful situation.

"Look, my old man just wants you to rest and get over your spell."

"You keep repeating that, over and over, like it's something your father told you to say. And if that's true, where's my wallet and phone?"

"He musta taken them to see if he can find you some help. Find your family. I bet he's calling them right now."

"I don't need his help. I just need my phone to get my own help."

"Suit yourself."

"What does that mean?"

He refused to say another word.

Chapter 30
Abit

I WAS GOING CRAZY with so much time on my hands and nothing to do but eat and sleep. I lay on my bed and tried to settle my mind, the way the counselors at The Hicks taught us to do. I waited and waited for some kinda calm to wash over me. I was about to give up when in my mind's eye I saw those ponies, the wild ones in Mt. Rogers and the New Forest ones too. I lay there thinking about them and remembering what they'd taught me.

Be kind.

I hadn't felt kindly toward anyone in what felt like forever. That led me to thinking about Baldy and how he should be outside, running round full of mischief. Instead he was washing dishes in a cellar, wearing his little apron like a good boy, doing someone else's bidding.

At that moment, one of my favorite prayers came to me—*help me be a little better person every day*. Something about "little better" made it doable. Strange as it sounds, I knew that meant showing Baldy some kindness. *Not* his old man, mind you, whoever he was. Just his boy. I didn't know exactly how to pull that off, but at least I could quit sniping at him. He wasn't the reason I was stuck there, lying on a flimsy bed.

When I rolled over, I could see Baldy sitting at his table, staring directly at me. "What?" I asked.

"Tell me about your boys."

Like the way grief keeps you connected to loved ones who've died or left you, talking about those you're separated from makes them feel closer. I was bursting with stories and pent-up thoughts. How Conor was already a gifted fiddler, and Vern was more of an outdoors kid. He loved the creek and fishing, but he also spent a fair amount of time in the kitchen helping me or Fiona with a meal. He'd even baked some bread.

"I can cook too," Baldy chimed in.

"Yes, you can. You do a fine job with the meals."

"I'd do more, but my old man says we have money problems, and I tend to waste food, you know with mistakes and such. But, of course, that's not a problem in the States."

I couldn't help but laugh. "Not true. I don't know anyone who doesn't worry about money."

"Yeah, but my old man says you Yanks worry about swimming pools and stocks and bonds, and we worry about food and clothing."

"I think someone's been watching too many 'Beverly Hillbillies' reruns."

"Huh?"

"Oh, never mind. That's just not how things are back home. You likely have no reason to study Appalachia, but we're poorer than most people in your country, though I'm sorry you have money troubles too."

"Do your boys get an allowance?"

"Yeah, but not a big one."

"How much?"

"A dollar a week."

"What's that in pounds?"

"Not even one."

"Oh." That seemed to stop him. He messed with his model a while, then put it aside. "Tell me another story about them."

"Last summer, the boys were kidnapped by a madman." I left off the part about the serial killer. I didn't want to give him or his old man any ideas.

"Oh, come on. That's a big porkie" (aka *lie*).

"No, I'm serious. And it took the FBI—I think that's like your MI5—to get them back."

"You're making that up. That's telly talk."

"Well, it's no more unbelievable than the fact that you've got me locked up in a cellar, against my will." But this time I said it more like stating facts, not hurling hate his way.

He thought about that a while, then nodded. "You know, you don't seem like a bloody Yank."

"Well, I am. A Yank. But I'm glad I'm not a bloody one, in all senses of that word."

As we talked, I could feel my distrust of him ease; I thought the feeling might've been mutual. That got me thinking about how when I was a kid, I felt better when someone from outside the family was inside our home. Like the two workman who came to make our kitchen more modern. I told Baldy about it. "They spent several days working inside, and something about having outsiders round our house made it feel safer."

Baldy started nodding his head up and down, like he knew exactly what I was talking about. When I looked directly in his eyes—wary, sad, with lashes so small they couldn't keep a speck of dirt out—something changed for me. As he was agreeing, with a smile so faint I wouldn't've called it that if I hadn't spent so much time with him, I couldn't help but see myself in him—complete with a lousy father, crazy mother, and nobody to play with when I was his age. It was like looking at *me* some thirty year ago.

"Did you have many friends?" Baldy asked. He was gazing at his feet, not able to look me in the eye. A wave of sorrow washed over me—both for him and me.

"No, not really. I kept to myself." He was nodding again. "But to be honest, I didn't try very hard. I was too scared people would say no. I had short friendships with people like those workers I just told you about, and this hobo who set up camp in a meadow behind Daddy's store. And I had a kinda friendship with a girl, Annie Totherow. She was so fine-looking, her long blonde hair going down her back in a soft braid. Her father delivered honey to Daddy's store, and she'd sit on the bench and talk while he was inside, doing business. But no, no friends until Della Kincaid bought the store and moved in above it." I coulda gone on forever about Della, but I stopped. "And my friend Duane Dockery—he and I ran the Rollin' Store together."

"What's that?"

"Folks in our county live so far into the middle of nowhere, the store comes to them. Or I should say *came*. It's long gone now, but it was an old school bus when Duane and I took it out; early on it was just a wagon pulled by a horse."

"I'd hate not getting to go down the shops."

I was glad to hear he got out of this cellar sometimes. I supposed when the coppers weren't trying to find him, he went to school and lived a somewhat normal life. I hoped so. "How about you, Baldy? What are your friends like?"

"Uh, yeah, I've got friends. Like you just said." I knew enough to leave it at that.

He seemed lost in himself after our chat. Thinking about not having friends will do that to you. To cheer him up, I told him about a chair that was a friend of sorts. "I loved that chair. I'd found a butt-sprung caned chair thrown out behind the store. I pulled out all of the old cane and fixed it up with woven strips of inner tube. That made it real comfortable, especially when

I'd lean against the wall. I could sit for hours like that, just watching people come and go from the store."

Baldy jumped up and ran to a spot in his room I couldn't see. I heard him rummaging round, and after a while, he held out an old straight-backed wooden chair with a hole in the seat. "Like this one?"

"Close enough." We both smiled at the idea of us having matching chairs. I didn't have the heart to tell him I'd lost track of that chair some fifteen year ago, though I'd have to look for it when I got home. *If* I got home.

He went back to searching for some kind of rubber or inner tube, but came up empty. I looked on my side in the crap corner with all the junk, but no luck. I did find some string, so I stood over by the jail wall and used that to show him how to weave the seat and secure the ends round the framework. "Just ask your daddy to help you get ahold of an inner tube. I know you've got them here in England too."

Baldy got a rag and started cleaning the cobwebs and dirt offa the chair. That night, when I lay on my bed, I pictured him sitting in his own chair, or leaning against a wall, pondering life. I prayed it'd be a better life than this.

Chapter 31
Abit

I FELL ASLEEP AGAIN. To be honest, it felt good to sleep this much. When I woke what felt like hours later, there was more food. Delicious spaghetti Bolognese. Better than last night's supper, or was that lunch? Baldy's old man was a good cook. At least I reckoned it was his old man. Could've been his mother, for all I knew. Whoever, the food tasted better than even the Bridgewater Arms with its fancy chef.

After a while, I saw Baldy go over to the sink and wash the dishes and put them in a bin with handles. I hadn't noticed that before, and there was a well-practiced system to all this that worried me. When he finished and returned to work on his model ship, I watched him slip back into being a boy. No toughness, no bossiness, just a young'un caught up in a fun project.

That twisted up my insides. It killed me that his youth was being stolen, stuck down here in some dank cellar, doing what he was told. And it didn't sit right, either, thinking Baldy had anything to do with the Ownbey gang.

I stood and started walking round the room just to get my legs moving; my muscles were cramping from so much sitting and sleeping. Baldy put down his model and watched.

"Just getting a bit of exercise," I said.

"No you're not. You're looking for a way to escape. I saw you last night, doing silly buggers with that lock." I felt my face burning. "Give it up. There ain't any way out."

"Isn't."

"Don't start that with me."

I recalled how Della, so many year ago, helped me learn to talk better. But that wasn't my job; Baldy wasn't my kid. Or my friend. I needed him only to get me outta there. I kept walking round, and Baldy finally got up. "You'll never figure how to get out. I don't even know. My old man said that is for the best."

"And you believe him? That living here is for your best?"

"It's only for a few days. Till the coppers give up looking for me."

"Look, what's really going on here?"

"We've been over that a million times."

He ignored me after that.

"Wake up. You're snoring."

"I don't snore," I said.

"That's what they all say."

They? "Who is *they*?" I barked and added an expletive.

He winced at my swearword, and I started to laugh. The first time in what felt like ages. And it felt good.

All the fussing about swearwords made me think of a fellow I knew back home. Wallis Harding. "I've got a friend who doesn't like to swear either," I told Baldy. He tried to act like he didn't care, but I could tell he did. "He makes up his own swearwords, using combinations like you've never heard before."

After a long pause, he asked, "Like what?"

"Oh, funny things, like son of a biscuit and crappity, crappity, crud. Oh, and oyster shucker."

That caused a slight upturn of his lips, but then he got real serious-like. "Wouldn't everyone know what you were *really* saying?"

"I guess some folks would. It's hard *not* to think what they're referring to, isn't it? But there's no harm. It's funny." That made me think of something we did as kids. "I don't know if you ever do this here in Blighty, but when I was your age, we'd go round saying things like Hoover DAM, putting extra oomph on the *dam*. Of course, we just wanted to say that word."

"What's Hoover Dam?"

"Oh, don't tell me you don't have dams here in England. You know, big walls of concrete that hold back water?"

"Oh, I get it. Like our Kielder Water." Which of course didn't work with saying *dam*, but Baldy kinda smiled anyway. Then he stopped abruptly. "I couldn't do that. My old man would just say that everyone knows you're still thinking a dirty word."

"I know I've said this before, but your old man has his nerve acting all holier than thou about a few swearwords when he's kidnapped me, holds me against my will in this dungeon, away from my family. And keeps his kid stuck in the same dungeon, waiting on me, and for all I know hiding a gun to keep me here." I pulled my shirt away from my chest. "And I've lived in these same clothes until they stink." (I'd been trying to stay clean in my small bathroom, but there's only so much you can do with a little sink.)

Baldy walked over to a cupboard, opened it, and then stuffed a large, well-worn t-shirt through the door slot. I'll tell you, I was grateful for it. Until I held it up and saw the letters on the front: WANKER.

"Really?" I asked, holding it out to him. Baldy just shrugged. I thought about it for a beat, then pulled off my dirty shirt and tugged WANKER down over my chest. It fit. Beggars can't be choosers. I wadded up my old shirt and threw it in the junk corner. I didn't care if I never saw it again.

I thanked him for the shirt and picked up where I'd left off. "Look, I'm sorry about your lousy home life. As you may have figured from our talks, I know all about that. But I've gotta get outta here. It feels as though I've been here for weeks."

He'd gone back to his model ship and didn't look up. "You need a hobby."

"I have plenty of hobbies—at home, where I want to be."

"Hang on, hang on. It won't be much longer."

I laid down, not believing him for a minute. I stewed about things for a while, and then, as I was drifting off, I finally knew what I had to do.

Chapter 32
Della

I HEARD MY CELLPHONE ring, and I hurried to the back of the store to catch it before it went to voicemail. I grabbed it in time, but I couldn't make out what the person on the other end was saying. Screaming like a banshee was the expression that popped into my head, which made me think of Fiona. If she was calling from Ireland, it could only be bad news.

"Hold on, Fiona. I can't understand a word you're saying."

A long transatlantic pause before she composed herself. "Abit's missing."

"What do you mean missing? Isn't he there with you and the kids in Dublin?

"He went to see that eejit, Nigel."

"Oh, that's right. He's in London. Did you call Nigel?"

"I tried, but the number I have has been disconnected. I remember Abit saying Nigel had moved somewhere, but I've misplaced his new number. Abit's been gone for three days, and we've hardly heard from him. The boys are missing him." She had a way of punctuating the end of a sentence with the verbal equivalent of a foot stomp. "Then I got these texts from him. You know how Abit hates to text, so it seemed strange. It *is* strange. He wrote that he'd gotten himself in 'a spot of bother' and needed five thousand U.S. dollars. I ignored it. Figured it was some kind of scam like you read about. I'm trying to keep the boys, well, *us* from worrying, and I hoped you'd heard something."

"No, I haven't heard from him." I grew alarmed when she admitted that she'd ignored some earlier texts. "What did the other texts say?"

"They were weird with flowerdy words to try and sweet talk me. Nothing like Abit would write, so I ignored them. We were busy, having a good time with my family." I'd met her father and sister at their wedding, and I didn't think Abit was missing much, but maybe that was unfair. Anyway, she went on, "I thought it was a joke of some sort."

Of course Abit didn't send those texts, but after the second one, she shouldn't have ignored them. I wanted to read her the riot act, but she was already in banshee territory, and I didn't want her scaring the boys any more than they likely already were. "Tell me more about the latest text and how you responded."

"Let me find it on my phone. Hold on a minute ... Here it is. There's the thing about saying he needed five-thousand U.S. dollars, and oh, he says don't call the coppers. I wrote back, "You need to call me if you think you have a prayer I'll send that kind of money to you."

I knew Fiona was tight, but this was a new low. I'm glad she didn't give away their hard-earned money, but her cavalier attitude angered me.

"I don't know any more details, Della. I just hoped you had Nigel's new phone number."

"The only number I have is a London exchange." I heard her go into a swoon, and I quickly added, "Okay, sit tight. I'll do some work on this end and get back to you. I *will* find Nigel." *And then I will kill him,* I thought. I quickly added, "And Abit!" but she'd already hung up.

I waved at Annie stocking the locally made section and hurried upstairs, Rascal racing ahead the way he does. I found my contact information for Nigel easily enough—but it was his London number. Then I remembered Nigel had called me a month or so ago—wanted my advice about some fool idea he had. When I checked my cell phone, though, I couldn't find the call anywhere in my history.

Alex was back in Chapel Hill. I left a message on his phone to come home ASAP.

I was starting to panic.

Chapter 33
Abit

I NEEDED TO KIDNAP BALDY.

I wondered why I hadn't done that when I had the chance during our lunch together, but this sorta thing was so outta my ken, I'd needed time to get my thoughts together. I'd been avoiding thinking too far in front of me, refusing to even consider where all this could be heading.

Of course, I wouldn't really hurt him—just hold him hostage like they were holding me. With my size I could easily overwhelm him next time he unlocked that door. Tie him up with torn bedsheets. Threaten him and tell his old man when he came downstairs with his stupid shepherd's pie that he needed to let me go—or else. As I lay on my back on my bed, I imagined how the whole thing played out.

"What're you smiling about?" Baldy asked. It wasn't until then that I noticed he'd moved his worktable close to our shared wall. I must have been asleep when he did that. I was so surprised I didn't say anything. He waited a bit before asking again. "I *said*, what are you smiling about?"

I looked over at him, a young boy working with everything he had on a model ship no one else would likely ever see. And just like that my idea fell apart. I couldn't harm him or even pretend to. He'd had a rough enough life without my violent threats, imagined or real. I didn't know how I was gonna get out of the cellar, but I would. Just not that way.

That stirred a recollection of something I'd read. How people who'd been kidnapped grew close to those who took them. I reckoned I'd joined that club.

Chapter 34
Abit

WHEN YOU'VE DONE ALL you can do and find you're going round in circles, that's a good time to give up. And I did. Not just my crazy, even violent, ideas but *everything*—all my worries, all my threats, all my anger. I believe the right word is I *surrendered*. I turned it over to Jesus and asked for his help. I'm a big believer in "pray to God and row to shore," but at this point I reckoned I'd rowed as far as I could go. I'd studied the room, and it appeared to be impossible to get out of. I'd begged Baldy to help me and tried a little kindness (though even I was aware of how pathetically short-lived that was). I'd hollered at his old man with lame threats, and I'd thought up a scheme to hurt a little boy that made me sick to my stomach. I couldn't go much lower. All I could do was lie there on that sorry bed, sleeping or killing time. I had no idea how this was going to end, but I was through trying to figure that out.

I finally felt easier, and I wanted to do something besides eat and sleep. And maybe because Baldy'd reminded me I needed a hobby, I got up and stirred round in that corner with all the junk and found a few small pieces of old wood. When Baldy was busy with his ship, I slipped the paring knife out from under my mattress. It was awful dull, so I rubbed the blade against the sharp edge of my metal bed. That helped a little, good enough to whittle.

Baldy glanced over, curious-like. After a while, he stood to get a better look. I held my breath, afraid he'd take the knife away.

"Where'd you learn to do that?" I let out a sigh of relief. He seemed more fascinated by my carving than the fact I had a knife.

"Oh, here and there. It's almost like learning to walk back where I grew up."

"Which was where again?"

"The mountains of North Carolina—a state in the southern U.S. People there have to make things for themselves more than other parts of the country."

"Do you make things for your boys?"

"I've made a lot for Conor. I think the bear was the best one. But not so much for Vern. Like I said, he just came to live with us a year ago. I haven't had time yet."

"You carving that for Vern?"

"More than likely."

Baldy unlocked the door and came over close to watch. I liked showing him what I was doing, though after a time, his snuffling really got on my nerves. Then outta nowhere the thought that I could slit his little throat flashed through my mind—but just as fast I felt ashamed.

I ran away from those thoughts by talking. I started jabbering on to Baldy about Laurel Falls and our house on the hill and how when I was just a little older than him, I'd sit in my chair and whittle outside of Daddy's store.

"You would've liked it there. We had a bench, and a bunch of regulars would just hang out. Kinda like a pub but without refreshments. Unless they went inside and bought a Dr. Pepper or something. That's like a Coca-Cola only with a more cherry-like taste. Anyway, I whittled some dogs and bears and squirrels, but I gave them all away."

"I've never seen a bear."

"Really? You don't have bears in England?"

"Not since 1,500 years ago. I learned that in school."

I chuckled. "I bet you did."

"What're carving?"

"Wait and see."

Chapter 35
Della

"WELL, LOOKY WHAT THE cat dragged in."

"Good to see you too," I told Sheriff Horne.

He chuckled, motioning for me to sit in the chair opposite his desk. "Just a figure of speech."

I got lucky—he appeared to be in a good mood. I noticed he wasn't wearing a tie (he was usually pretty buttoned-up about dress code), and he had his feet up on his desk, looking more relaxed than the last time I'd seen him. It had been about a year since he'd broken up with Mary Lou Dockery when she took up again with her ex-husband, Duane Dockery. I was never sure if they'd remarried, but they were still together. Things in small towns are always intertwined.

"Okay, I'll bite. What brings you to Newland."

"I need a favor." I'd realized he could help out after all. And he owed me. I'd done some computer research for him a couple of months ago, and I was about to call in my chit.

"Well, of course you do. Why am I not surprised?"

"Is that what I said when you needed a favor not that long ago?"

"No, no you didn't. You said something like go take a long walk off a short pier."

I laughed. "But then I helped you."

"So who said I won't do the same?"

He was right. He hadn't said no, but I'd gotten my back up as though he had. I knew I'd better tamp down the sarcasm if I expected to get what I needed. "It's Abit. He's in trouble over in England. Actually, he's missing."

"I don't think the county would approve my going over there to look for him, but I sure would like to try." He chuckled again and actually tossed some peanuts in his mouth.

"Listen here, Horne, this isn't funny. He's gone missing, and I know he wouldn't take a walkabout on his own. His family is in Dublin, and he probably didn't want to leave them in the first place, other than the fact he was looking forward to seeing Nigel Steadman."

"Oh, say no more. That scoundrel attracts trouble like a dog in heat attracts ..."

I held up my hand to stop him from finishing. "You're right about Nigel. But I'm talking about Abit."

Horne finally turned serious. "What can I do to help?"

I explained about Nigel moving from London, and no one this side of the Atlantic knowing his new contact information. "I got a call from him about a month ago, but I can't find it on my phone. I believe that call came from his new phone."

"Probably a burner, knowing that guy."

"Maybe. But maybe not. It's the only way to get ahold of him without going to the police over there. I don't know what kind of mess he's gotten Abit into, so I don't want to go that route. Yet."

He thought a while and asked if I had time to go to a café to talk it over more.

"I already ate a ham sandwich at my desk."

"Yes, and I believe you had Dijon, no mayo." He was smirking again, looking at my midriff.

"How'd ..." I looked down and saw a big splat of brownish yellow on my blouse. I smirked back.

"Hey, no need to feel embarrassed around me. My tie's in the bathroom drying from the same ingredient." He closed his laptop, grabbed his keys. "Let's go to Lottie's. I need a coffee, and you can tell me more about how I can help."

Chapter 36
Abit

THAT NIGHT I SLEPT more peacefully—until Baldy had a nightmare that woke me from a deep sleep. I was groggy, but I believe he was crying out, "Mollie, Mollie." Made my heart hurt—for his longing and mine. We both got back to more restful sleep, and I didn't wake till I smelled the aroma of bacon.

Without windows, I was getting all confused about the time of day or even what day it was. That was another thing the old man had taken from me: my watch. But the meals did seem to be regular-like, and this was the third breakfast I'd had there. Next I'd be marking the walls like they do in prison movies to keep track of the days.

I had no complaints about the breakfast. It seemed that in spite of my troubles, my appetite held strong. I had to hand it to him or her: Whoever did the cooking here knew how to make a fine half-English. That may sound obvious, given I was in England, but not everyone here knows how or still cares enough to do them proper-like.

I could see Baldy tuck into his food, and I felt something deep and sorrowful. When he was wiping some toast round his plate to get the last bits of egg and banger, he caught me looking. "What?" he asked with a belligerence I'd hoped we'd gotten past.

"Oh, nothing. Just thanks for another good breakfast."

He nodded and began carrying his dishes to the sink. I passed mine to him through the slot. "What's going to happen to me? How's this going to end?"

"I told you. No one's going to hurt you. My old man is putting out feelers."

"Why doesn't he just let me go? I can creep back to my hotel at night. I'm good at that sort of thing. And by the way, I feel stupid calling him your 'old man.' What's his name?"

"Cyril." Baldy wiped his hands on a towel and walked over to resume work on his model ship. I could see it much better now that he'd moved his worktable. He was doing a fine job of it, and I felt a strange stab of pride. Then outta the blue, I had another violent fantasy of me getting ahold of his model somehow and smashing it to bits with my hands, then dropping it on the floor and stomping on it. I was up and down and all over the place, but tell me, who wouldn't be?

That was how things went. Back and forth. One day same as the next. In the end, I was so bored I asked Baldy if we could trade stories.

"Okay, but no porkies this time. They have to be true. I don't want you feeding me a bunch of lies."

"Who said anything about lying? Besides, you and Cyril are the liars. Keeping me trapped here with fake reasons."

"You're the liar."

"Am not," I said.

"Suit yourself." Baldy turned away from me.

"Okay, okay. Yes, no lies."

I told him about the capers Della and I got up to in Virginia and Washington D.C. How we caught a trio of con artists and how I helped Della find a little girl's mother. When I mentioned I took pictures of her mother embracing another man, Baldy got red in the face.

"What a load of rubbish. I said no lies."

"I'm telling you the honest truth; these things really did happen. At first I couldn't believe them myself. Me, Abit Bradshaw, stupidest kid in the school, traveling the East Coast to run down scofflaws."

"What's that? And don't call yourself stupid."

"Scofflaws? You know, no counts, crooks, whatever you call them."

"I don't call them anything. I don't hang out with people like that."

Ha! First off, I knew Cyril was someone like that—as were Clive and Ian and all that gang. But then I reminded myself I was over that, right? This was just about me and Baldy making the time pass. "Okay, tell me one of your stories—and no lies."

"I'm not the liar here," Baldy said, though I swear I saw a flicker of a smile. I nodded for him to go on. He got this dreamy look and started talking about his mother. They used to live in Brighton, he said, and his mother worked at a really nice restaurant, so they had money for fun things along the pier and the seaside. "We went to the pictures every Saturday, and then we'd get ice cream on the pier. I loved living there."

"What did your mother do at the restaurant."

"She was one of the cooks—they called her a sous chef."

I figured she must be the one upstairs doing the cooking. The whole family was in on this. I held onto that thought and asked Baldy when they'd moved to Ringwood.

"Huh?" He'd been lost in a favorite memory, and I was sorry I'd interrupted.

"I said when did your family move to Ringwood?"

"When she left."

Chapter 37
Della

"Steadman." Nigel answered on the first ring.

"Where is Abit, Nigel? And don't do that dancing-around-the-facts thing you're so good at." I knew I was going about this all wrong, but I didn't have the patience to be nice. "Where is he? Fiona called me in tears because she got a crazy text from him about some kind of extortion, and she doesn't know where he is."

"Well, er ..."

"What Nigel?"

"We, um, lost him."

"We?"

"Oh, let's not get into that, Della. I've done it this time. We've been looking everywhere. We need to work together to find Abit."

"No kidding, Nigel. Fiona is getting nonsensical texts from him, or rather from his phone, asking for five thousand dollars. He says he's in a 'spot of bother,' an expression that has your name all over it. Are you shaking down Abit's wife?"

"Well, I never! I thought we were friends, Della Kincaid. Do you honestly think I'd do that to the lad?" He sounded so contrite, I almost let up.

"We are. And no, I don't really think you had anything to do with that. But the point is, we need to find Abit, and you're useless at finding things—other than trouble."

"Hold on. Hold on. Everything was going along very well, and then ..."

"What do you mean 'everything'?"

"Er, well, Abit was helping me with something."

Nigel brought me up to date with Abit going undercover for him and Nigella, whoever she was. No doubt some paramour who'd broken the law somehow. I knew this guy. And when he rambled on and on about poor Nigella, that's when I lost it.

"Stop it, Nigel. Abit is the one who matters here, not some tart named Nigella, which for heaven's sake, would be like me having a boyfriend named Dellan or Delaney." Unfortunately, I carried on about that and his unspeakably mixed-up loyalties until I heard a click followed by the dial tone.

I supposed I'd deserved that. I tapped the recall button, but just as quickly ended the call. Instead, I headed to my computer to make a reservation for Heathrow.

Chapter 38
Abit

AT FIRST I THOUGHT Baldy meant his mother had left, like a divorce or separation. But something about the way he was sitting there with a long face and sad eyes made it clear she'd left for good. I just sat quiet-like, waiting to see what lies he told to get round this.

He was in the kitchen, messing round with the kettle, not at all his usual practiced self. I could see him getting the teapot ready when he accidentally knocked a cup offa the table. It crashed to the floor. He actually swore.

I knew better than to call him on his curse when I saw how he cradled the broken pieces of that nice ivy-patterned cup in his hands. As he looked straight at me, his lip started to tremble.

"What's going on, Baldy?"

"Nothing!"

He didn't say anything else till he brought my cuppa to the door slot. When we were both seated on our separate sides, he finally spoke. "That was the last cup I had from my mother."

I could feel his sorrow, but I knew it went deeper than a cup. After a while he said, "Look,

I *have* been peddling a pile of porkies," his lip trembling again. "My mother's gone. She's not a lunatic or a drunk and never was. She was lovely—but she left us. Me."

For the longest time, neither of us knew what to say. I finally broke the silence. "But why are you down here in this dungeon if you're not hiding from your mother or the coppers?"

"What else am I gonna do?" he said. "I'm nine years old. I do what the old man says."

"Then tell me why I'm down here. You can trust me." He just shook his head, looking awful scared and confused. "Let's get outta here, Baldy. Come with me. You don't have to live like this."

"Yeah I do. If I run away from the old man, they'll just put me in care—like your Vern woulda been. You know what I'm talking about."

I did.

WE TALKED ON AND off throughout the rest of the day, though Baldy seemed distracted, like he was working out something in his head. His cockiness was gone when he asked, "You really wanted Vern, didn't you?"

His question tore at me, so naked about his own needs. "Oh, yeah. And Conor too. Their mother and I are crazy about those boys." I wished I hadn't laid it on so thick about how much we loved them, but it was too late. When

Baldy turned his head away, the light caught a tear stealing down his face and dripping onto his striped shirt. And anothern.

"I'm not sure what's really going on," he said after a while, snuffling more than ever. "I just figured I should stay with my old man. At least I know him. Better than the devil I don't know."

He had me there.

Chapter 39
Della

EVERYTHING WAS HAPPENING SO FAST, I felt dizzy from the noisy crowds, garbled announcements, and yellow-and-black signs plastered all over Heathrow. I sat down for a moment, but then a security guard came by and told me to keep moving. When I made my way through customs—I'd brought only a large backpack, so I got through quickly—I found a café and stopped for a cup of tea and sandwich. The tea was disappointing. I'd been longing for a cracking good cuppa, but it tasted tepid and old. Fortunately the crusty baguette sandwich—Cheddar, Branston pickle, lettuce—was delicious.

I texted Alex that I'd arrived safely. It was only yesterday I'd left him in charge of Coburn's. He'd made it back from Chapel Hill in time to drive me to Asheville to catch my flight. I'd had to pay a fortune for the ticket, but I figured that's what money is for. Besides, I'd always wanted to come back to England, though
not much hope of any sightseeing this time.

It wasn't a great time to leave the store, but I trusted Annie, and Alex agreed to look over the video recordings nightly. Knowing him, he'd turn it into a research project, like the good journalist he is. Who knew? Maybe Mr. Pulitzer would watch the boring videos every day and discover something I'd missed. Even as tired as I was, I laughed out loud remembering Alex's face when he'd realized I had video recordings of my customers.

"You mean you've had camera images for weeks now?" he'd asked on the way to the airport.

"Yeah, Candy Man." I'd discovered via the videos how he'd helped himself to candy bars in the store whenever he was in town, that sweet tooth of his leading him astray. He had a good laugh about getting caught, not the least bit embarrassed. But then I wouldn't want him to be. He knew he was welcome to them.

I RENTED A CAR at Heathrow and headed down to the New Forest. When I'd been to the U.K. before, I'd never driven on those visits, too afraid of driving on the left. But with Abit in trouble, I didn't give it much thought. I just drove. When I got to Lyndhurst, it was easy to locate the hotel where Abit had told Fiona he was staying.

But I didn't like what I found.

Chapter 40
Abit

THAT EVENING, I WAS LYING on my bed when supper arrived. I leaped up, but to no avail. Whoever was delivering stayed safely behind the heavy door, never saying a word.

A few minutes later Baldy passed a plateful to me. The heap of fish and chips barely fit through the slot. As soon as we'd sat at our own tables, we both dove in. It was even better than I'd had on my jaunt to Stonehenge. At least I knew Baldy was getting good home cooking—even if it was short on fresh vegetables. And my spirits brightened when it came to me that surely they wouldn't feed me so well if they were going to kill me.

When we'd each finished, I asked Baldy if there was any birthday cake. He looked at me like I was crazy. I'd tried to make it sound like a joke, but I wasn't laughing. "It's my birthday today," I said. "At least I think I've kept track of the days down here. Thirty-seven."

"Oh!" Baldy said and went over to a cabinet where he dug round in a coupla drawers.

Eventually, he came back with something small in his hand. When he stuffed a crumpled packet of Walker's shortbread through the slot, he said, "I wished I'd known." I wanted to raise my head and howl at the moon over such innocent tenderness. As I opened the packet, I could smell how old the biscuits were, but I acted pleased. I was.

Not long after he'd done the dishes and settled in with his ship, Baldy looked over toward my side and asked, "Why'd you stop carving?"

"I finished," I answered, acting like that was the end of it. His face registered such disappointment, I couldn't pretend very long. "I thought you'd find it—down there, somewhere below the slot on your side."

He walked over toward the door, past where I could see him, but I could hear him snuffling as he looked round. "I don't see it."

"It's wrapped in a napkin."

"What?"

"I mean a serviette."

He was muttering to himself, but in time I heard, "Ah!" He stepped where I could see him unroll it. "Why'd you put it there of all places?" I could tell he was trying to act cool, but I sensed his anxiousness.

I waited a beat longer. "It's for you, Baldy. I made that bear for you."

He stared at it like it was a rare gemstone, rubbing his fingers over the faceted wood I had no way of sanding. "What about Vern?"

"I figured I'd have time this summer to make him one. I've still got a glimmer of hope that I'll get to go home."

He was quiet as he turned the bear over and over in his small hands.

Chapter 41
Della

NIGEL WAS SITTING IN the pub at the Bridgewater Arms knocking back what looked like a gin and tonic.

"Get off your sorry butt and find our boy!" I shouted like an ugly American. I didn't care if everyone in the pub stared.

"Er ... a ... Della what are you doing here?"

"What do you think? What's happened to you, Nigel? You once brought such joy into my life, but lately you're more like a dark shroud. What have you done to Abit?"

"Nothing, it was Clive."

"Who in the world is Clive?"

"Long story."

"I'm waiting."

Nigel told me he was "shattered" that Abit had been nabbed. He gave me the Cliff Notes version of Clive Ownbey and his gang, adding that Abit had helped them trace the stolen goods, which would hopefully mean the police would have to release Nigella.

"That woman again. Listen to me, Nigel. If you value your life, you will never, and I mean never ever, use that woman's ridiculous name again. I didn't fly all the way over here to worry about her or even you. If you weren't such a self-absorbed pillock you wouldn't be here sipping a G-and-T. You'd be out looking for Abit." By then my fury exploded into a lapel-grabbing episode, wrinkling his custom-tailored suit coat as I pulled him off the bar stool. "If that boy has been hurt ..."

"Uh, he wouldn't like you calling him a boy," Nigel said in a cowering way, doing a very good impression of Stan Laurel.

I pulled myself together and let go. I thought about everything good about my boy—I could call him that in the privacy of my own thoughts, though Nigel was right. He'd earned the right to be called a man years ago—and started straightening Nigel's tie, patting his lapels, trying to ease the wrinkles. "And besides" he added, "this is only tonic and lime."

I sighed. "We need to find Abit."

THAT EVENING, I MET the club and felt an immediate connection to Marcia. Not so much Graham and Malcolm. And Roy Arthur Lewis? Had to admire his chutzpah with that air-conditioned hat and a cravat, for heaven's sake. Fortunately, Marcia took the lead.

"We've been looking high and low for dear Abit. He helped us connect with Ian McCafferty,

Clive Ownbey's wingman, and he risked his safety on two occasions to reconnoiter round their safe houses." I thought of Abit's and my capers in Virginia and D.C., and my heart ached.

"And he plays a cracking good mandolin," Roy Arthur chimed in.

After they filled me in on what Abit had been up to, I asked what they had done to find him.

"Well, we didn't know he was missing, did we? Not until yesterday," Graham answered, his livery lower lip stuck out in a gesture meaning "So there."

"I'll repeat my question. What have you been doing to find Abit since *YESTERDAY*?" I heard my voice rise rather sharply on that last word.

They looked like a bunch of kids caught smoking behind the school. I gave up for the night. "I'm tired. Long day. Let's meet here for breakfast to plan what we *all* can do to find Abit." I turned and almost ran upstairs to my room.

Nigel followed, uttering little mewling noises that made me want to hit him. I didn't. Once we were in my room, though, I let it fly. "You entrusted our boy to those idiots?" I growled, my hand pointing down through the floorboards, as though he didn't know where they were.

"Hang on. Hang on. They're my friends."

"And you, me, Alex, and Abit are more than friends. We're family. Remember?" Nigel sunk onto my bed, where *I* really wanted to be right now. "I need some sleep. I'm being a shrew. See you in the morning."

I didn't grab his lapels again, but I did push him out the door.

Chapter 42

Abit

"DID YOU EVER READ to your boys?" Baldy asked late that evening.

I bit back saying *of course.* I didn't want to make him feel even more left out of a world of love and kindness. The way he'd asked told me everything.

"Yes, and I sometimes still do. When they're all keyed up after a concert or a nightmare. I even read to my wife, Fiona, sometimes. It's a nice thing to do." I paused, hoping he'd say something. When I looked over, he had this faraway look in his eyes. "Would you like me to read to you, Baldy?"

"Oh, I wasn't asking for me."

I nodded as though I believed him. "Oh, I know, but we don't have all that much to do down here. And you're almost finished with your model. What do you have to read?" I was hoping it was something I could keep reading after our session was over.

"Not much." He looked round and moved some things on a shelf. "Oh, wait, here's something." My spirits brightened till he added, "The instructions to my model ship."

I was about to spit out a snide comment, but then I knew it didn't really matter what I read. If that sounded exciting to him, it was okay by me. He slipped them through the slot.

Baldy seemed to naturally know that he needed to get under the covers, and I pulled a chair from my dining table closer to the wall. As I read to him about glue and paint and sails and masts, I put everything I had into it. I lifted my voice when it talked about the joys of model making, and got serious-like when it cautioned not to use too much glue. When I looked over at him, I could see him working the satin edge of his blanket like Fiona sometimes worked her rosary, and I figured those two things weren't all that different. He looked at peace. And happy.

I worried we'd get to the end of the instructions without anything else to read. I could always make up a story, like I sometimes did for the boys, but to be honest, I didn't have it in me.

Didn't matter. On the last page, close to the bottom, I looked over and his eyes were closed. Even his snuffling had stopped.

I turned out my light and quietly slipped onto my bed.

Chapter 43
Della

Jetlag felt like moving underwater in slow motion, yet I couldn't rest. I'd tried, but all I could think about was Abit. I still wanted to go to the police, but as Nigel reminded me, they didn't get serious about missing persons (or mispers, as he called them) until three days after they'd disappeared. Well, that was now.

I was so off schedule, I didn't know if it was lunchtime or dinnertime, but I was hungry, so I ordered a ploughman's from room service before heading out to retrace Abit's steps on the last day anyone saw him. When it arrived under a silver dome, I was already predisposed to love it. I marveled at how such simple fare could taste so good, especially with the real ingredients at the ready.

I started my search in Abit's room at the inn. I was grateful Nigel's deal with the owner extended Abit's stay so all his belongings were still there, at least as far as we knew. Nothing offered even the slightest clue. Then I asked Cilla, the front desk woman, if she recalled where he'd gone that day. She directed me to the high street, and I wandered around in a fog. I had a picture of Abit in my wallet and showed it to shopkeepers and tearoom owners. At the third tearoom, a young woman said she thought she remembered him buying something to take away. "Yes, I definitely remember, though I'm not sure which day he came in. But I wouldn't forget that red hair and sticky-out ears." I wouldn't mention that to Abit when we found him. And we *would* find him.

When I got back to the hotel, Nigel had left me a note that he was "at the scene of the crime." That meant the Dog & Bone. I was glad to have a chance to check out that place. According to Marcia, Abit had spent a lot of time there talking with gangsters and playing music. Maybe someone knew *something*.

I got directions from Cilla and drove a bit too fast, and to be honest, on the right side of the road for a short time before I saw an oncoming car. I arrived safely. When I walked in, Nigel was, where else, hanging around the bar. I sat down and ordered a G-and-T. "I've been wandering Lyndhurst's high street, Nigel, and all I did was confirm that he'd been there. It's pointless. If we haven't found him by tomorrow, I'm going to the police."

"Della, I'm telling you, *don't*. These gangsters mean business. Clive Ownbey is one of the worst. Why do you think we've been tiptoeing round him? He's smarmy, one of those hyper-polite crooks that make your skin crawl. Next to him, that idiot back in Laurel Falls seems like, oh, I don't know, Paddington bloody Bear."

"Johnny Ray Meeks. He was plenty smarmy, though minus any courtesy. See what I mean, Nigel, about the kind of people you attract?"

I pouted a while. Nigel ignored me. Then he got off his barstool and walked over closer to the bartender. They had words, which I couldn't hear. The bartender put his hands up in a "meant no harm" gesture.

I sipped my drink and waited. "What was that about?" I asked when Nigel returned with some kind of clear liquid.

"I didn't like the way that bloke was listening to everything we said. Did you see him? His neck stuck out like an ostrich?"

"I believe they stick their necks and head in the ground."

"Yeah, but when they're above ground, they do what I just said." Nigel nursed what he'd told me was a tonic and lime.

"Learn something every day." I wanted to ask about his temperance, but that would have to wait. I had an idea.

I got up and ordered another G-and-T, for purely undercover reasons, and while the barman was slicing the lime, I asked him if he'd ever seen this kid. Nigel was right; he *was* the nosy type, and he might prove helpful. Maybe he'd heard something between Clive's gang and Abit.

I flashed my wallet picture like a copper showing a badge, and I saw him flinch. Probably brought back bad memories of when he really was looking at a badge. He was a big guy, rough looking, and likely had a checkered past.

"Yeah, he'd be hard to miss. Tall feller. Played a fine mandolin too. I see a lot of musicians here, and he's one of the best yet."

I knew Abit was good, but he seemed to be laying it on pretty thick. "Any idea where he might have gone? Did you hear him talking with Ian McCafferty or his sidekick Toby?"

"Oh, sure, but they were just having a chinwag about this and that. Nothing that would explain his disappearance." He wiped the counter before adding, "I've seen a lot of tourists come and go, and there's no telling what gets into their heads. He's likely gone down to Bournemouth to see the seaside or up to Stonehenge."

I thanked him and told him to put my G-and-T on Nigel's tab. Nigel looked up and gave a wave to let him know that was okay.

"I don't like that guy one bit," I growled when I was out of earshot. "And he flinched when he saw Abit's picture."

"Is it a good picture?"

"Not particularly. Why?"

"Maybe he didn't like Abit's looks."

"Oh, come on, Nigel. He's a great looking guy. Just ask Cilla."

"What about her?"

"I can tell she's got a crush on Abit. She let me know she'd do *anything* to help us find him."

"Okay, okay, he's a great looking kid. So why did the bartender flinch?"

"That's *my* question. And then he started piling up the false flattery about what a great mandolin player Abit is. I mean he *is*, but his praise was over the top. Like he was trying *not* to look suspicious."

Nigel grunted. "So what do you want to do?"

"Follow him home."

"DID YOU EVER GET his name?" I asked Nigel. We were sitting outside a Sainsbury's where we'd followed the bartender when the pub closed.

"No, I didn't, and unlike America, they don't all wear plastic nametags."

"Well, we need to name him something. I can't keep calling him the bartender. How about Barnard? Get it?"

Nigel grunted. "You know that means strong as a bear, and he looks the part. Keep that in mind."

Just then Barnard came out with several large bags of food.

"He's a big guy, all right, but that's still an awful lot of food," I said looking through the night vision binoculars. I really wanted a pair of my own, though in Laurel Falls what could I see at night? Raccoons? Skunks?

"Maybe he has a big family."

"I asked you to check on his background. I saw you sweet-talking the young woman doing table service. Why didn't you ask her what his name is?"

He ignored my question. "She said *Barnard* has a kid. Maybe a wife. But a kid can eat you out of house and home. Our conversation was cut short when she had to
run back to the kitchen."

Barnard pulled out of the parking lot, and we followed from a distance. He drove quite a ways into the forest then turned down a lane. I stayed back and turned off my
headlights. Fortunately, he soon parked in front of a small, one-story house. Modest looking, two bedrooms, maybe three. Stucco exterior with a bay window in
what was probably the living room. Nice enough, but nothing unusual.

I pulled into an area well away from his van, which looked like an old delivery van, converted for camping. Or kidnapping. After he lugged the groceries inside, we saw a light go on in the kitchen. A little later, that light went out and one came on in the back. Likely his bedroom. Was the kid asleep in the other bedroom? Didn't seem like much going on, but my gut was telling me to check it out. I fiddled around to find the rental car's interior light, turned it to the off position, opened the door, and eased out.

"Where are you going?" Nigel asked in a low whisper.

"To have a looksy. Just stay here." I didn't have to say that twice.

I used the flashlight on my cellphone to help as I crept along the side of the house. I had to pull myself up using the sill to see in the kitchen window. Major pots and pans in the sink. Must do a lot of cooking. The next room was dark with curtains drawn—again, made me think of his kid. I ducked below the next window with the lights on, and I got the sense he was doing all the things necessary to prepare for bed. Clothes off, night clothes on, bedsprings groaning, lights out.

I walked all around the house, relieved they didn't seem to have a dog. One little yapper could be heard in the distance, nothing that would send an alarm. I did notice the house had a solid underpinning, the kind that more often than not meant a basement. But without a window anywhere, I doubted anything was down there besides spiders.

Chapter 44

Abit

I TOSSED AND TURNED. Couldn't sleep. I just lay there, trying not to think too much. Then Baldy had another nightmare, only this time I was already awake, so
I heard him right. He was calling out, "Mummy, Mummy."

Later in the night or early the next morning, impossible to tell without windows, I woke to the sound of Baldy's wheezy breath. Even though I was turned the other way, I sensed he was standing over my bed as sure as if my back had eyes.

"Abit? You awake?"

I grunted something at him. I couldn't speak at that moment. I'd been dreaming about Conor and Vern, trying to find them down by our creek back home.

"It's time to go," Baldy whispered.

"Go where?" I managed to ask.

"Home."

Chapter 45
Della

AFTER OUR BUST WITH Barnard's stakeout, Nigel wasn't even listening to me. Finally I begged. "Let me do *something*. Go undercover like Abit did. Peep in windows. Follow people and rifle through their belongings. Back in the day I faced down some pretty scary mobsters on my crime beat."

Nigel still seemed to be ignoring me, but a short time later I realized something must have sunk in. "Okay, let's go back to one of those cottages Abit and I discovered," he said. "Ownbey's hangout. Tonight."

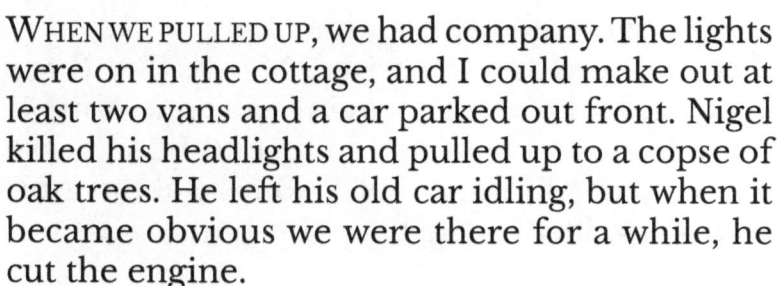

WHEN WE PULLED UP, we had company. The lights were on in the cottage, and I could make out at least two vans and a car parked out front. Nigel killed his headlights and pulled up to a copse of oak trees. He left his old car idling, but when it became obvious we were there for a while, he cut the engine.

"Don't you dare get out, Della." Nigel looked stern and unyielding.

I stayed quiet. For a while. "Come on, Nigel, let's go. Abit may be in there."

"We can't just go charging in."

"Why not?"

"Oh, you Americans."

"Oh, you Brits. Get on with it! Just go ask him."

"So how has that approach been working for you?"

"We'll see." I threw the door open and jumped out. The thought of Abit inside this dump, tied and gagged or worse, gave me courage to run to the side of the so-called cottage. I eased up to the window. The lights were bright enough I didn't think they'd catch me looking in the window, given how reflection works. They were all inside like a bunch of pirates, divvying up piles of loot ranging from pearls and other necklaces to rings and bracelets that sparkled with the real thing—diamonds. They were all laughing and horsing around.

Their levity made me so angry I lost any common sense I had and marched up to the door. I barged in without knocking.

Wow! Were they surprised. Me too. But there I stood, and I wasn't leaving without Abit. "I know what you boys are up to, and I don't care about your pilferage, but I do care about Abit Bradshaw. Just let me take him home. He's not a danger to you."

No one said a word. It was like those "Twilight Zone" episodes when life just freezes in place. After a minute or more, the man I assumed was Clive Ownbey swaggered over. He was pretty much what I'd imagined from Nigel's description: finely tailored suit, pocket scarf, small mustache, Brylcreemed hair. Not all that different from Nigel.

"I don't know what you're talking about." He crossed his arms in synch with a smirk spreading across his face. Like he was playacting. "So now that you've so rudely interrupted our little party, please leave."

"Not so fast, big guy. First Abit."

"I have no idea what you're talking about. I couldn't care less about some hayseed Yank."

"If you don't know anything about him, how do you know to refer to him—erroneously, I might add—as a hayseed Yank?"

His smirk turned into a full-scale smile.

"What's so funny?" I asked. "I'm serious."

"I can see you are. But I don't know anything about your friend. We don't have him in our dirty little clutches, as you Americans say. And if I did, I believe I *would* turn him over rather than spar with you."

"You're a liar."

"And I'll hand it to you—you're fearless. And *that* scares me." He made that gesture with his thumb and forefinger slightly apart before adding, "At least a little."

I knew he just toying with me, and at that moment I believe I honestly did want to kill him. But as his goons moved in, that notion dissolved into chills down my spine. I turned and ran.

I could hear laughter but fortunately no one followed me as I made my way across the uneven ground. I prayed I wouldn't twist an ankle—and that no one in the gang was a crackerjack sniper.

Nigel was waiting outside the car. "What are you doing just standing around?" I asked. "We need to get outta here." That's when he told me about the battery.

I was steamed about having to give his stupid car the crank of life, but the relief of being out of there and the plummet in my adrenaline soon left me limp. As we drove back to the pub, I told Nigel what had happened inside and how lucky I felt that Ownbey hadn't taken me as a serious threat. For once, chauvinism came to my rescue.

"I don't care what Ownbey did or didn't do to you," Nigel said, "I know they're guilty."

"They're guilty all right—of stealing a bunch of jewelry and valuable small objects." I told Nigel about their booty party, and I could see his shoulders relax. "So that's good for your ol' pal Nigella. But you know what? I didn't see McCafferty anywhere around that shack. I think it's time we had a talk with *him*."

Chapter 46
Abit

DARKNESS SWALLOWED ME WHOLE, yet I wasn't afraid. The cold, moist air felt intoxicating after that dank cellar, and the rustling leaves sounded like the prettiest music I'd heard in ages. I was so giddy with freedom that I wanted to hug the raccoons or badgers or whatever was scurrying in the night. Life!

Back at the cellar, Baldy had stood by the open door as I'd jumped outta bed. When we climbed the stairs that had brought so many meals to us, I saw there was another big door at the top. He'd already opened that one as well. He musta been a better lock picker than me. He put his pointing finger to his mouth, reminding me to be quiet. We tiptoed through a kitchen to a back door, not saying a word. He unlocked the deadbolt careful-like and pointed into the night. I silently begged him to come with me, but he just shook his head.

I hugged that boy like he were my own. And ran.

I wandered a while, lost in the New Forest. Eventually my joy began to fade as I grew more fearful. I didn't know where I was. I felt some relief knowing no one was following me, so I sat on a log covered in time-softened bark and listened, waiting for a sign. I heard scurrying and gnawing and then a hoot owl, but no great thunderbolts about what to do next. I thought about trying to sleep until daylight in the shelter of the log, but I had no way of knowing if morning was seven hours or seven minutes away.

I stumbled over brambles, shoots reaching out to capture me in their tangled net. I plunged ahead, fighting against anything trying to hold me back (though the scratches on my arms and legs burned like fire). I found a path and kept walking, more to stay warm than any idea about where I was headed.

I recalled my surrender earlier and tried for it again, but that's not the kind of thing you can fake. Besides, at that moment I knew I was no longer surrendered. No, I *wanted* to see my boys, my wife, my dog again. Thinking of them, knowing I was closer to being with them than I had been for days, my heart pounded so loud I almost missed it.

A sound.

At first I reckoned it was just the leaves again, whispering a different song now that the winds had died down. But in a little I heard it again, and this time I knew what it was. Whinnying and nickering. My friends the ponies.

I headed toward them, hurrying, afraid they'd stop. I made my way through the forest unaided by any moonlight (the sky was blanketed with thick clouds), walking careful-like toward their musings. As I grew closer, I could tell they were engaged in a responsive chorus: calling, answering, calling, answering. With a few more steps I began to see their wooly shapes.

I'd been so excited about finding the ponies again, I hadn't stopped to consider how they could help me. Other than not feeling so alone in the forest, so what? I was still cold and lost.

The ponies drifted away as I neared, more afraid of me than the night. In a while, one started nickering. That was when I heard a different horse answer, off in the distance. They carried on like that for a while until it struck me. Yes, that horse a ways off could be in another herd of wild ponies, but maybe, just maybe, it could be one of the Travellers' horses acting as the sentinel, the way horses do.

I bid the ponies good night and wandered in the direction of the distant sounds. Eventually, I saw the flicker of a campfire. I couldn't believe my ears when I heard a fiddle. For the second time that night, I began to run.

Chapter 47

Della

"I STILL THINK THAT BLOKE knows where Abit is."

That was Nigel. He'd finally put his full attention on finding Abit—now that he'd learned Nigella had been released.

Apparently Abit's and the rest of the club's efforts had paid off. The cops had enough on the Ownbey gang for the theft of the jewelry as well as other larceny. Not to mention that I'd called in an anonymous tip once I'd caught my breath after cranking that blasted car.

Most of the club members reconvened at the Dog & Bone, just hanging around because that was where Abit was last seen. Nigel put out feelers for Ian McCafferty, but it was Marcia who finally located him. He'd agreed to meet with us.

While we waited, more news trickled in from mysterious sources of both Nigel and Graham. Apparently Clive had stayed above the fray, his soldiers taking the fall for him. I can't imagine what that must feel like—having people doing your bidding, no matter if that included prison or even death. Of course, to pull that off, you had to be a completely disgusting person, so I didn't think I'd try it.

Barnard either had the day off or worked a different shift. Whatever, I ordered a coffee—one of those Rombouts coffees pubs serve. I had just finished it when McCafferty walked in. Nigel ran over and cornered him. No hands on lapels or anything like that. Just close.

"Nigel, I didn't know you knew that lad until yesterday," I heard Ian say with irritating calm.

"That's a lie and you know it. Abit told me you asked about me, and that was four days ago. Four days of worry and waste."

"What? Sending in boys to do your dirty work now?"

"He's a man, McCafferty. Thirty-seven years old yesterday." That was me.

"And who might you be? Is there some kind of Yank convention going on?"

"Yeah, there is. And there will be more coming if we don't find Abit Bradshaw soon." Of course I was lying, and of course he knew it.

He smiled and raised his arms like cowboys do in westerns. "Okay, pardner, I've got my hands up."

That was when I kicked him somewhere painful. Not too hard, but I was sick and tired of people treating this like a game. I believed Nigel was about to step in for a double whammy when McCafferty backed up, getting out of range.

"Okay, okay, I get it. This is important to you." Ian caught his breath and went on. "I met that kid, and I really liked him. But I don't know where he is, and I didn't kidnap him." As Nigel and I both moved toward him again, he quickly added, "But I think I can help you find him."

Chapter 48
Abit

As I GOT CLOSER to the Travellers' camp, the horses were carrying on like a pack of guard dogs. I hid behind a tree to get my wits about me. I was pretty sure this was the same camp where Nigel bought his car—and the dodgy battery. As I was thinking how to handle things, I looked down and saw that my shirt screamed WANKER. I turned it wrong side out, hoping REKNAW didn't mean something awful in whatever language they spoke.

As I eased forward, I saw four men standing in different places pointing some kinda long-barreled guns into the forest. They were calling out to one another in their language, and oncet they'd gathered together, they started walking toward the woods, guns forward. I held my breath and stayed behind a tree. I didn't dare move or they'd hear the crackling of leaves underfoot. They couldn't see me, but I knew I couldn't stand like that forever. I needed their help. *Please dear Lord*, I prayed, *don't let me find freedom only to get shot!*

"Come out and show yourself. We see you there," someone shouted in English with a heavy accent.

I came out with my hands in the air, shivering so bad I could barely walk straight.

Some younger guy started motioning me with the gun, the way they do in movies. This wasn't the first time I'd had guns pointed at me, and I knew firsthand what a bullet could do.

"Uh, I don't know if this helps or not, but I came by here with Nigel Steadman and bought a car from you. A nice little Morris Minor." Needless to say I didn't mention the battery rip-off.

"I don't know what you talk about. Or why you creep round our camp. You're not welcome here."

No kidding, I thought. "I'm lost."

The men now surrounded me, guns pointing at various parts of my body. They walked me slowly toward the fire, which I welcomed, given my lack of warm clothing. I was hoping to sit round the fire while they figured out what to do with me. After that run in the woods, I felt awful tired. It didn't help, either, that I'd spent a full week lying on a bed and eating too much. In spite of being in prison, I musta put on five pounds.

We stood there for what felt like ages. Finally, the guy in charge shouted at me, "Get down on your knees." I did what he said and somehow kept my arms raised without falling on my face. "Now explain yourself."

"Danior, for heaven's sake, put that gun down. This is my friend, Abit." It was Theodosia, the woman who'd served us tea and scones. "Danior, you are as hotheaded as your father. Not everyone is our enemy. See." She pulled on the lapel of her jacket to show him something. I think it was the pin I'd given her, the one to remind her of her mountains back home in Romania. Danior nodded and lowered his gun. The other three followed.

"Now come with me, my boy. It's too late to take you home. You can sleep in one of our wagons."

She led me to the wagon with all the curlicues painted on it. I was so excited to sleep in one of their colorful wagons I felt like a kid Baldy's age. Theodosia fussed over the bed, pulling it back for me. I lay down, put my head on the soft pillow, and I swear I fell asleep that moment.

I slept the sleep of the dead. I could hear the sounds of morning work and breakfast making, but I kept turning over and going back to sleep. The feather mattress felt like heaven after my prison bed's thin mattress. It was after noon when I finally stuck my head outta the wagon.

"Oh, there you are, Abit. I take it you sleep well." Theodosia was making tea, and I was gasping for a cuppa. "I make you breakfast. Get washed and dressed over there. I found new shirt for you. WANKER not right for your homecoming."

I wasn't sure which shirt I'd rather show up in. The one she was holding out for me had puffy sleeves and a bright red swirly design painted on it. At first I thought they were flowers, but on closer inspection I could see they were birds. That was something, at least.

I slipped the shirt over my head and pulled it down. When I turned round I saw Theosodia walking away with my old one, holding it at arm's length, the way you do when you've picked up a dead mouse. I gobbled down the bread she'd made in her dutch oven; she'd also laid out some dried meat and blackberry preserves. I ate everything in sight.

Just as I was finishing my second cup of tea, I saw Danior and Silvanus, the battery thief (and who I later learned was Danior's father) walking my way. Theodosia clucked her tongue at them, like Mama used to do to let folks know she meant business.

"Where can we take you?" Silvanus growled. I could tell he didn't like having to help me. Gone was the man who spoke so kindly to Nigel when he was buying the car.

"I used to have a hotel room in Lyndhurst. At the Bridgewater Arms. I don't know if they've saved it for me, but I'd like to go there."

"That is long way for us to go. I've asked round, and it seems you were playing music at the Dog & Bone in Ringwood. That is closer.

That is where we go. You will know someone there to take you farther. We are not welcome everywhere." I realized then why he'd been so grumpy—he didn't want to leave the safety of his compound.

"But first," Danios said, extending his hand, palm up. I thought he meant friendship—like he was apologizing for pointing a gun at me, but then he started rubbing his thumb over his first two fingers, letting me know he wanted money. "We need to be paid."

I heard more clucking from Theodosia but to no avail this time. His hand never wavered. I tried telling them I had money in my room in Lyndhurst, but they knew as well as I did that could be long gone. With those two guys glaring at me, I sighed with relief that something I'd done before we'd left home hadn't been so crazy after all. Even Fiona didn't know about it. I'd taken the heel offa both my boots, carved out a hidey hole, and stashed two twenty dollar bills in each boot before replacing the heel.

I needed a hammer to get the heels off, and I didn't know how to ask them for something they might see as a weapon. So I took my boots off, told them about the heels, and handed one to Danios and one to Silvanus. "Knock these heels off and take the money inside. And hurry up, my feet are freezing." I was feeling braver with Theodosia looking on.

The two men looked at me like I was trying to pull a fast one, but I gave them a look right back that said *take it or leave it*. They took it. I reckoned $80 U.S. dollars was good enough, because they loaded me in an old truck—in the back, of course—and we headed to the Dog & Bone. I waved at Theodosia as we passed by. She threw me a kiss and held out her lapel with the pin catching the midday sun.

Danios and Silvanus stopped the truck just as the pub came into sight. "You can walk," Danios barked outta his rolled down window. I wanted to say *And you can go to ...*, but then I had to admit, grumpy or not, they had helped me.

I felt foolish in the fancy shirt, especially since I'd need to ask for more help in the pub, but the warm sunshine and birdsong made me mostly forget about it. I walked into the pub and saw the bartender wiping down the bar. Gosh, it was good to see a familiar face! I gave him a cheery hello.

He gave me a dark, no make that menacing look. What? Had I not paid my tab last week when they carted me out after someone slipped me a mickey?

"How did you get here?" he spat out.

"Uh, well, the Travellers gave me a lift."

"Not that, you daft git."

Where had I heard that before? Someone else called me a daft git recently. Just then I heard a customer call out to the bartender, "Hey, Cyril, we need another round over here."

The penny dropped.

"Holy Moly, you're the 'old man'!"

I didn't feel as strong as I did a week ago, but I had muscles to spare compared to this flabby, overweight slob. (No wonder he had those extra pounds, given how good a cook he was.) I flew across the bar and tackled him as he headed toward the men at the end of the bar. I saw them scatter as I took Cyril down. He didn't know what had hit him.

By now everyone in the pub had gathered to watch the brawl. More than likely they were already taking bets on who would win as Cyril and I went round and round, twisting over one another. Someone was trying to pull me offa Cyril, but I wasn't having it. I shook him off and gave Cyril a hard jab for every day I lay on that stinking bed, and then a started on a few for Baldy's sake. By then it took several men to wrangle me away from him.

When they finally stood me up, I heard, "Look! It's Abit!" That would be Nigel. The start of it all.

Then a copper put handcuffs on me. As he led me outside, I couldn't believe my eyes. Della Kincaid.

For the second time in one week, I passed out.

Chapter 49
Abit

I WOKE UP IN PRISON again. This time it was the local police station in Ringwood. When I came to, I was in a cell, but then they moved me to an interrogation room, where after a long irritating beep, a couple of coppers—a man and a woman—spoke into a recorder, announcing who was present, the time and date, and all that. The only thing missing was Cyril.

"Where's that fat Cyril?" I asked.

"Sir, we're not in the habit of bringing in *victims* of crimes."

"VICTIM?"

"You assaulted Mr. Ownbey."

"Ownbey? I never touched him."

They looked puzzled. Sure, crooks always said they were innocent, but you could tell they thought I was outta my mind.

"Are we talking about Clive Ownbey?"

They nodded to one another, like they understood now. "No, Cyril Ownbey."

"Are they related?"

"Brothers."

"And you trust *his* version of the story more than mine?"

"We have witnesses that say you jumped over the bar and gave Mr. Cyril Ownbey a major thrashing."

"I did, indeed, and here's why. He held me captive—and his boy, Baldy, I want to add—for the better part of a week in a dungeon!"

I wished I'd chosen a different word than that last one. I knew I sounded completely mad.

"You may have a solicitor present, Mr. Bradshaw."

"I don't want one. I want Cyril present so we can straighten this out. You can't let him get away. He's probably halfway to Liverpool by now. Or wherever you go to leave this country! I know that's where I'm going as soon as possible."

"Sir, that is not going to happen. Now calm down and tell us in your words exactly what transpired."

And I did.

Chapter 50
Abit

DELLA WAS WAITING WHEN they finally let me out—after the coppers offered a mild apology. Nothing you could take to the bank, but still, they seemed to feel bad that I'd had such a hard time in their country.

We hugged like it had been two years instead of two weeks. She held me back and looked me over, her eyebrow raising the way it does. "Nice shirt."

"You shoulda seen the other one."

We walked round to a café next door and grabbed a table by the window. "Just sit tight and save this seat for us," she said before heading to the counter. "You probably want a view of the outside world and a bit of British sunshine after your ordeal." She came back with two cups of tea and a large French roll with something in the middle.

"I thought I'd let you eat first," she said. I nodded, my mouth full. It had been a long time since Theodosia's breakfast. What I thought might be cheese was a horrible-tasting paste I only just managed to swallow. I was about to put it aside when I realized that when I finished, I'd have to tell her everything that happened, so I munched round the edges. After two hours with the coppers, I'd come to realize how hard this whole mess was to explain.

After a while, I did set the awful sandwich down and got up to get us each another tea. We both sipped a while, like two old friends enjoying a cuppa together. We were, but we were also about to discuss the latest caper we'd been through together. I finally got up the nerve to start. When I'd finished, she still didn't say a word. "What? You don't believe me?" I asked.

"No, Honey, I do. What you just told me is pretty close to what Nigel figured. After you were carted away, he and Ian captured Cyril. They held him at the Dog & Bone in what I assume is the British equivalent of our citizen's arrest."

"Ian? Ian McCafferty?"

"Yeah. Interesting guy. I guess there *is* honor among thieves, what with him helping Nigel."

"Helping? And how did they know to hold Cyril?"

"I believe they trusted you, Abit. You know in spite of his nefarious ways, Nigel was beside himself about what had happened to you. Ian came up with a plan, and he and Nigel have been out looking for you. Something to do with Barnard, er, I mean Cyril. Turns out he's Clive Ownbey's brother, trying to be a tough guy like his big brother but in such a pathetic way."

"I know. The cops just told me. I'm glad I didn't know that when I was in the cellar. Not that I knew it was Cyril, but you know what I mean. Did Nigel know they were brothers?"

"Not until the coppers told him. Apparently, the brothers were estranged. Clive was ashamed of Cyril. I guess the big-time gangster was embarrassed by the penny-ante crook. Not felonious enough to maintain the family reputation."

"And that's why Baldy didn't know anything about *Clive* Ownbey." I sipped my tea and added, "You know, you sure got all the facts in a hurry."

"That's what us reporters—even former reporters—do."

"Well, I'm glad they're on to Cyril, but what about Baldy? He took good care of me this week."

Her eyebrow went up again. "*Took care of you*? Abit, he held you captive."

"No. No. He was just doing what his old man told him to do. He's only nine year old."

I still felt unsettled about why Ian was helping out, but suddenly flashing lights filled our window as a coupla cop cars pulled up outside the police station. Two cops hurried outta the first car and opened the back door. Della and I nodded with satisfaction as Cyril slowly worked his way outta the car and perp-walked down the sidewalk. When I couldn't see him anymore, I stood and went back to the counter for more tea and two pieces of Victoria Sponge.

The cake was dry and stale, not even a distant cousin to the one Marcia shared with the club one afternoon. I'd been on a good run with British food, but it had come to a screeching halt in this place. While I was hacking away to get at the part with raspberry jam, another car with flashing lights pulled up. Next thing I knew, Baldy got out—not in handcuffs, but still a disturbing sight. When I started to knock on the glass window, Della grabbed my wrist. "Honey, don't."

"But he's scared, and no one's there to console him."

"I'm sure they'll take him into foster care once they talk with him. And his father."

"That's exactly what he's scared of! He told me over and over he didn't want to go into care. He's just a lonely little kid!"

We sat there a while longer before Della suggested we leave for the Bridgewater Arms. "Nigel told me that's where you were staying, so I got a room there too. Really nice place. Actually, Nigel got me the room. Says they owe him."

"They must owe him big 'cause that's what he told me too."

"Let's not find out what that's all about, okay?"

CILLA RAN OVER AND hugged me when we walked through the front door. Della gave me another raised eyebrow, but I ignored her.

"Oh, we were so worried about you, Abit." Cilla said, kinda breathless.

"Yeah, thanks. I was too."

"We've saved your room for you—no one's been allowed in there—except her." She nodded Della's way. "Everything should be in order."

Della and I went to our rooms. I changed my shirt the minute I closed the door. I folded it careful, though. I reckoned I'd hang onto it, just because.

I laid down on the comfortable bed with crisp white sheets and slept hard. It was late in the day, almost suppertime, but I needed some rest. I was wore out from all that had happened.

I woke when Della knocked on my door. "See you downstairs for dinner, Honey," she called out. I could hear her walking away before I could answer. I cleaned myself up, put on a plain shirt, and headed to the dining room.

Della had dolled herself up for dinner. She looked so pretty sitting at the table, I almost didn't recognize her. Not that she didn't look good most of the time, but back home, we don't bother with dressing for dinner.

We each ordered a pint (Strongbow Cider for Della, Old Speckled Hen for me), and I asked about Fiona and the boys. "Have you heard from Fiona? I hope she hasn't been worried."

"You don't know the half of it," Della said. She sensed my worry and added real quick-like, "She's fine now. I already called her and told her we'd found you and all was well. You should call her tonight, though."

It's a terrible thing to say you dreaded calling your wife, but I knew Fiona would read me the riot act, saying all the usual about Nigel. I'd been hoping she was having such a good time she hadn't noticed I'd not been sending any emails. Didn't sound like that was the case. When Della filled me in about the weird texts Cyril had sent Fiona, I knew I was really in for it.

Then Della caught me up on news from back home. Mollie was fine, Shiloh was Shiloh, and the store had some kind of mystery of its own going on. Just as she started to tell me about that, Nigel walked in, dressed in a suit even I knew cost a bomb. The guy had style, I had to give him that. When he announced the meal was on the house, Della and I just looked at each other; over the years together we'd learned to say a lot without speaking a word.

So I ordered the most expensive thing on the menu—lobster, something I'd never had before. I expected Nigel to raise a ruckus, but he just laughed. The sweet, delicate meat dipped in butter tasted so fine, I almost wished I hadn't ordered it, since I wasn't likely to ever have it again. On the side, some kind of baked dish of thinly sliced celery root was almost as good. We did have those back home, but we usually threw them away; I'd give them a closer look next time. Della got beef Wellington and Nigel Dover sole. No wonder we didn't say much for a while, tucking into our meals.

During dessert, Nigel explained some things for us. (By the way, I got the Eton Mess. Figured that was a fitting name after what I'd been through. Meringues all broken up with fresh strawberries and whipped cream. Doesn't sound all that good, but it made up for that with each spoonful.) He told us five coppers came into the banquet room at the Dog & Bone where he and Ian had been holding Cyril to keep him from doing a runner.

"They talked to Ian for a while, and then he left," Nigel said. "They grilled me a lot longer, but it seemed Ian's story backed up my story, which backed up yours, Abit. That's why they released you so abruptly. Oh, and back when your room got tossed? That was Cyril's doing."

Nigel went on to tell us how the coppers had Cyril show them the way to his house, though his brother, Clive, had already given Nigel the address. Said he was thinking of Baldy, hoping Nigel could get there before the coppers. But they'd already sent a team round to the house. They took Baldy to the station, like we'd witnessed.

"But Baldy had picked the lock on that door upstairs. He coulda gone anywhere," I said. I couldn't believe the poor kid hadn't run for his life.

"You'd think he'd've left, but the coppers said he'd been cleaning in the cellar. There was a big pile of dishes drying on the drainboard, and they found him working on the bathroom in your area. It was like one guest had checked out, and he was getting the room ready for the next."

My insides twisted again thinking about Baldy scrubbing away in that awful place. Then something Nigel'd just said hit me. "What do you mean—*ready for the next*?"

Nigel looked round the nice restaurant. "Abit, I know this is going to upset you, but please don't make a scene."

I couldn't imagine what he was about to tell me, but I nodded for him to go ahead.

"Cyril did this to others," Nigel said.

"I knew it! The way Baldy seemed so practiced sometimes. And when he'd mumble, 'This never happened before.' Okay, so those other men can back up my story and put Cyril away for good."

"Well, there's a problem. So far they don't have a clue about where to find the other victims of Cyril's scheme. There's evidence he extorted them, but the victims aren't traceable. It's up to you to put him behind bars."

"And I will!" I barked, banging my fist on the table. Some heads turned.

"Good lad. Yes, good." Nigel looked so funny, I wondered what he hadn't told me. "You know that means Baldy will be put into the foster system." He didn't even know Baldy, and he seemed sad about that. I hated to think what that program was like. I could hear Baldy crying out about not wanting to go into care as if he were standing right there in the restaurant. I felt shook.

Nigel waited a beat before adding, "But I have a plan."

"I bet you do," Della and I both said at the same time.

AFTER DINNER, WE WENT into the backroom where we'd held some of our club meetings. Sure enough, Marcia, Graham, Roy Arthur, and Malcolm were all there. Even Alfred and Roger. A couple I'd never seen before stood off to the side, holding hands with their backs to us. When they turned round I saw the pinned-up shirt sleeve. Had to be Miles and Nigella.

In my mind's eye, I'd seen Nigella as a sweet person, like Marcia. Turns out she was a real firecracker. Dyed red hair piled on her head, low-cut dress fitting pretty tight, and a laugh like a dying crow. She was acting all snuggly with Miles, and that whole scene just irritated me beyond words. All that trouble because of *her*.

Nigel introduced us, and I tried to remember my religion. If not kind, I was at least polite through gritted teeth.

"Oh, sorry, Abit. You got in a right mess all because of me." She slapped me on the back, and then pulled me into a hug. She reminded me of Miss Kitty from "Gunsmoke" but with a lot less class. Her perfume was fixing to knock me over when she let go and held me out in front of her.

"It's all that old Clive Ownbey's fault. It started when I pulled a fast one on him a year ago. Remember that, Miles?" Miles's face turned beet red, and he looked about as happy to be there as me. "He was just getting his revenge. And that was so dear of you, Miles, to defend my honor, pulling a gun on him. I doubt it did much good, but it's the thought that counts. You were defending my honor, weren't you?" Miles nodded, but without much enthusiasm. "Oh, and thanks to you, Abit, and Nigey (*Nigey?* I turned so she couldn't see my eyes rolling) everything got cleared up. Did they tell you I stayed in a four-star hotel? That was some jail. I wouldn't mind going back—how about you, Miles?" He studied his shoes.

"Uh, I don't get it," I mumbled. "You weren't in jail?"

"Oh, I was at first. But several things happened to change their minds. Once they realized I hadn't stolen anything, they figured they could use me to flush out the Ownbey gang."

"And use Abit, without his knowledge or consent." That was Della, stepping into the circle. I knew her so well, I could see the tendons in her hands tighten, struggling not to strangle Nigella. "All he wanted was a nice vacation." She glared first at Nigel, then Nigella, before turning and leaving.

I'd just spent way too much time stuck in a room with a sad little boy, so I hung round a while longer. It felt good to be out and about with adults—and beer. I mostly talked with Marcia—she was definitely my favorite—and we got a little drunk together. Well, I did. Marcia didn't drink. I asked her about what foster care was like in England, and it sounded pretty much like back home—a toss-up as to whether the kids got a good home or not. I knew whoever looked after Baldy would be lucky to have him.

"You know, Abit, you're not like any Yank I've ever known."

"Well, I'm not a Yank, not the way you all mean. Or a lad. Or a boy, as I've been called endlessly on this awful trip. I'm just a man who lives in the mountains of North Carolina in the United States of America."

Chapter 51
Abit

"COME ON, ABIT. THERE'S something you need to do."

Nigel had pulled his Morris Minor up to where I was sitting at the front of the inn, enjoying the flowers and sunshine. I was surprised he'd shut it off, but I was done helping him crank it.

"What about me not wanting to get involved in any more of your schemes didn't you understand?" Which reminded me of my phone call last night with Fiona. She'd said pretty much the same thing, only stronger. But I could tell she was happy I was safe, so that was something.

"Maybe I put that wrong," Nigel said. "The bottle and stoppers want to see you again." I sighed and got in the car. It started without the crank. Nigel caught my surprise and chuckled. "I finally bought a new battery."

We drove a while through the forest. Eventually, he turned down a lane and pulled up at a house. "Is this where I think it is?" I asked.

He nodded. It was the first time I'd seen it by daylight from the outside. You'd never know it had a dungeon inside. We waited a bit for the coppers to show.

"I'm sorry, Abit, that another visit with me has led to mayhem."

"Yeah, remember the good old days when I'd just stop by your apartment in D.C. above Firehook Bakery? Those were the best times we had together. Oh, and our visit to Churchill Arms."

"Yes, where I convinced you to phone Fiona."

That again. "Okay, I believe you've worn that one out. But no more. I've paid for that ten times over."

Nigel looked kinda sheepish, but he was saved by a car pulling up behind us. When a man got out, I recognized him as the copper I'd seen Ian McCafferty talking with at the Dog & Bone. I wanted to ask Nigel more about Ian, but now wasn't the time. Turned out the copper was a detective—DCI Rodney Kelly. We shook hands and then walked up to the house. He banged hard on the front door, and a police woman answered. She ushered us inside.

The upstairs was new territory to me, except for that middle-of-the-night exit in the dark, so I was handling it okay. I didn't get the jitters till we moved past a bookshelf that had been moved to one side. I knew then that was how Cyril had hid the stairs leading downstairs—and why Baldy'd said the police looking for him would never know about the cellar.

When we made our way down the steps, Nigel asked me how I was doing. I said fine. I wasn't. This was a sorrowful place long before I got there. I felt bad that Baldy lived in this house without his mother, who'd gone off and left a fine lad to the mercy of Cyril. I walked round the room, but nothing jumped out at me. I noticed the model ship—and instructions—were missing, so that eased my misery a bit. Then I remembered the bear I'd carved for Baldy. My heart started pounding when I saw the napkin I'd wrapped it in, just lying on the table, kinda bunched up. I picked it up. Nothing there. He'd taken the bear to wherever he was headed next.

"I want to go. I've seen enough," I said. "I'm not sure why you brought me back over here anyway. I've already given my statement a hundred times."

"Just procedure, sir," Kelly said. "We need you to take a look around. Let us know if you see anything else of importance."

"The only thing that went on down here was the crime of a boy being imprisoned so his good-for-nothing father could try to get money outta unsuspecting folks like me. Probably because the pub didn't pay him enough in the first place." I thought about that for a moment. "No, he probably coulda earned some good tips, but he's a miserable sort and no one would ever want to give him a penny extra."

DCI Kelly just nodded. Then he asked, "What about this cabinet, sir?" He was pointing at a small door under the sink.

"What about it?"

"Did you or the boy open this cabinet?"

"I don't know. I mean I know *I* never opened it. The kitchen was Baldy's territory. And no, to my recollection he never opened it. Why?"

"There was a gun there, sir. We found it once we had a warrant to search the premises. Did he ever attempt to use that against you?"

I just shook my head, too troubled to speak. I'd thought from time to time about my life being in danger, but until then it hadn't really sunk in how much. After that I just kinda poked round, only because DCI Kelly seemed to expect it. The place was clean as a whistle, the little tyke having made a good job of it. I did find my stinking old shirt, but I kicked it deeper into the corner. I saw the chair Baldy had cleaned up, ready for some strips of inner tube. Maybe someday he'd get a chance.

I felt sick with sadness as I spoke to the copper. "Nothing I see will help you any more than what I've already told you. I was kept captive here for four days, fed well, the boy cleaned up afterwards. That's all I know. I don't want to spend another minute here."

Chapter 52
Della

I HAD A PLANE to catch the next day. It left so early, I needed to spend the night near Heathrow. I still hadn't had time to tell Abit what was going on at Coburn's, and Nigel had just told me something about Baldy that I dreaded sharing with him. But that could all wait until he got home. He'd had enough tumult for a while.

I'd turned in my rental car—I was tired of driving on the wrong side of the road—so Nigel was taking me to the Salisbury station. When he pulled up in front of our hotel, Abit came outside.

"Okay if I tag along?" he asked. As if he had to ask. He still seemed shaken after his ordeal, not at all himself. He didn't say much until we pulled in front of the rather plain brick train station. "I wish I could hop on a train to Liverpool and get on the ferry to Dublin right now."

"When are you heading over to Ireland?" I asked.

"Tomorrow, if nothing happens between now and then." We both looked at Nigel, and he pretended he hadn't heard that. When we got out of the car, Abit grabbed me and gave me a big hug. "Thanks for coming all this way to help me," he said as he held onto me longer than usual. I hugged him back with an urgency that surprised me.

As he headed into the station to buy his ticket for the next day, Nigel and I both watched him walk away, stronger than both of us combined. My train was leaving soon, but I had just enough time to tell Nigel I needed him to keep me posted on everything—Abit, Cyril, Baldy. And I meant *everything*.

"Okay, but, uh, Della, I don't know the email, and I can't afford to call you that often."

There were enough people coming and going that I forced myself to tamp down my anger. I even kept my hands off his lapels. "Oh Nigel, after what you caused Abit ..." I couldn't find my words. I just wanted to mess up his hair and strangle him with his perfectly tied tie.

"Er, uh, I believe Marcia can help me," he said, adjusting his coat and tie even though I hadn't touched them. "I'll give it a go."

"You'll do better than that. You *will* learn it, and you *will* keep in touch until Abit is safely back in the U.S. and Baldy is settled in a good home. Got it? I want details—plenty of them so he'll quit worrying about that kid. Remember, I've got the goods on you, if I ever want to squeal on you. Think about that next time you decide to embroil my boy in your machinations."

He was nodding rather dumbly as I left.

I'd played a card I'd never wanted to—something from our past, back when I was a journalist. I'd kept him out of prison then, but I was willing to use that information to get what I could for Abit. I suppose the statute of limitations had passed, but at the very least I could make Nigel's life very uncomfortable.

Sixteen hours later, Alex picked me up in Atlanta. I was grateful I didn't have to catch a connecting flight to Asheville, and I looked forward to our time together on the long ride home. We had a lot to talk about. He wanted to know all about Abit, of course, but he'd also sent me an email the day before about something surprising on the Coburn's surveillance videos.

Chapter 53
Abit

THEY THREW ME A GOING-AWAY party that evening at the Bridgewater Arms, in part because I'd told them I didn't ever want to see the Dog & Bone again. I walked round, mostly on my own, trying to fit in and keep away at the same time. I was all mixed up.

It hadn't helped my nerves that earlier in the day I'd had to go back to the police station to give a formal statement. They told me I could go home (I hadn't realized that was even in question), but I'd need to send a deposition when the case went to trial. I sure was glad they didn't say I had to come back. I'd had enough of Blighty for the time being.

I stayed clear of Nigel, at least for now. I was glad to learn from Marcia that he really had gone on quite a hunt for me, but still, I couldn't help but think of him as the black sheep of our family.

Speaking of Marcia, she was at the party, as was Roy Arthur, his hat at a rakish angle that made me smile at his style—and courage. I chatted with them a while, and they both had gifts for me. Marcia gave me a package of English biscuits—bourbon creams, though as far as I could tell, they didn't have any bourbon in them. I'd be giving those to my boys tomorrow. Man, that sure sounded good. And Roy Arthur gave me a recording of an English band he was fond of; I looked forward to listening to it back home.

Marcia brought me a lager of some kind, but I barely drank it. I just wanted to leave this place. I wished I could fly straight home and meet my boys and Fiona at the Atlanta airport, but I didn't have the energy to broach that idea with Fiona or the airlines. Besides, heading to Dublin meant I'd get to see them sooner.

After the initial hubbub about me and how was I doing, I became yesterday's story. Everyone was carrying on the way they would tomorrow and the days after I'd left. That was fine by me. I'd have nice memories of Marcia and Roy Arthur, but honestly, that was about it. And, of course, Nigel.

I was surprised to hear a familiar voice. "Abit. It's been quite an adventure for you," McCafferty said. "Hope we didn't spoil your vacation."

"How can you even use that word? Vacation?"

"Okay, then a break from the busy life of a grocery magnate." He had a smug look on his face, which if I weren't trying extra hard to get back to my old self, I'd liked to have wiped off with my fist. And I wondered what in the world he was doing here. Why wasn't he in jail like Ownbey's other blokes? Or did he slip outta trouble the same way Ownbey had? He got a wicked smile on his face and said, "I had lunch with Della, and we talked about your tall tale."

After all I'd been through, I couldn't've cared less. I'd already come clean about my white lie of owning a grocery store chain. As if he could read my mind, he added, "Yeah, but if Cyril hadn't thought you were worth a fortune, he'd probably have picked someone else to extort."

Could this evening get any worse? Of course I'd thought about that and would likely spend more time on it in the months ahead. But isn't every word, every action in life a risk? A roll of the dice? And why wasn't he concerned about why Cyril was so mean to me and his kid and likely his wife and no telling who else? Those were the real questions.

Oh, please, just let me go home.

Chapter 54

Abit

June 19, 2006
Dublin Airport

I WATCHED AS CONOR AND VERN made their way down the walkway of the Dublin airport, more growed up than they were just days before. As they rolled their little suitcases behind them, marching forward with what surely was a swagger, I couldn't help but wonder what was in store for those two in the years ahead. I barely went anywhere beyond the farm and Laurel Falls, and yet my life had more twists and turns than the long road to Hanging Dog.

It broke my heart to see how sad Fiona was when we left Ireland. She was crying so hard at the airport, she fell into my arms and sobbed. She hadn't had much to do with me since I'd gotten back from England, except for lighting into me for scaring her so. But with all the tumult of leaving and packing and making connections, I thought that'd blown over. Then at the airport, I sensed a distance, even while I was holding her in my arms, my shirt all wet. It felt like she would've fallen into the arms of anyone standing close by, the way we need to lean on another human being—even a stranger—during a time of deep sorrow.

I was sorry our life back on the farm wasn't enough for her to look forward to. I knew that wasn't quite fair—goodbyes are always hard, especially when there's an ocean between you and the next visit—but something more was going on for her.

Even though the airplane was chilly, I felt sweat break out as I thought about my life, past and future. I knew Dublin was filled with the kind of life Fiona could never find in Laurel Falls, and there was nothing I could do except love her and help her settle back in. Wasn't it like coming face to face with work and school and life again after a peaceful camping trip—just on a grander scale? I could only hope.

The boys seemed quiet, too, leafing through dog-eared photos of Mollie and some new books their grandaddy bought them. Fiona had done a good job hiding my mess from them, so I hoped they weren't too upset by all that. I didn't think they knew much, though they might've heard Fiona reading me the riot act. She tried to blame me for ruining her holiday, but I wasn't having that. I was sorry for any worry I'd caused, but she didn't know the half of it. She'd had a great time with her family until the last day or so of my captivity; I'd had almost a week of bad times, counting the hours spent with the police afterwards. And we'd stayed a coupla extra days in Dublin so she could settle down and have a good ending to her time with her family.

It was a solemn drive home from the Atlanta airport, but I kept telling myself we were all just tired.

Part Three

Home Again

Chapter 55
Della

June 19, 2006
Laurel Falls, N.C.

"HONEY, IT SURE IS GOOD to see you again."

I'd lucked out. When I opened Coburn's on my first day back, Myrtle Ledford and Elbert Totherow were the only customers waiting to shop. I'd been gone only four days, but I was exhausted and just cranky enough that if some of the more difficult customers had greeted me, no telling what I might've said.

I'd noticed that Elbert came in more often now that Annie worked here. They were over in the honey department, checking our inventory when I responded to Myrtle's kind greeting. "I'd say it's good to be back, but I'm beyond tired. I'd rather be upstairs taking it easy." Even when I tried not to, I still sounded ill-tempered. I quickly added, "Not that I'm not glad to see you too."

"Oh, don't worry. I know what you mean. You must be done in from that trip—plus your other troubles … the bookkeeping ones Alex told me about while you were away."

I nodded and left it at that. She didn't need to know it was way more than bookkeeping. Alex had showed me the videos earlier that morning before he returned to his editorial duties in our more-than-cozy home office. He'd done a great job with the research, even strutting a little when he revealed who the crook was.

Before leaving for England, I'd spent hours going over those videos, but I'd never noticed anything beyond the comical pilfering by Alex and Cleva. Alex, on the other hand, was more careful. And he was less attached to the people in the videos.

As he told it, he was watching "miles of footage" upstairs in the apartment when the phone rang. He hit pause. While he was on the phone, he stared at the screen and realized someone had her hands in the pockets of an oversized raincoat. When he wound up the call, he hit play and watched her doing the deed. She also slipped two expensive bottles of wine into a cloth grocery bag. That inspired him to go back even further into the videos. He found enough pilfering to account for the majority of Coburn's losses.

We'd talked about this on the drive home from the airport, but I hadn't had time to come up with a plan. I wasn't sure yet how to handle things. Confrontation was usually my style, but I knew I should wait a day or two. Only I couldn't.

When the morning rush was over, I told Annie I needed to go upstairs. Rascal hadn't recovered from my sudden abandonment; he was sticking so close I nearly tripped over him as I climbed the stairs. I took them slowly after that, but not just because of him. I was dreading what came next.

I made a cup of tea, combed Rascal, made another cup of tea. When the only thing left to do was housework, I picked up the phone.

"Hi, Della. Good to hear from you."

Won't be after I say what I have to say, I thought. "Listen, something's come up at the store I need to talk to you about."

"Oh, did you forget where you put something? I've got a good memory for things like that."

"You've got a good memory, all right, but I think your forgot your scruples."

Dead silence. I waited several moments before going on. "Mary Lou, I've got you on video stealing from the store."

"When did you put up cameras?"

Not *I'm innocent*. Or *I can explain*. She was worried about cameras. "Doesn't matter. You're on the videos stuffing your bulky raincoat with all kinds of MY MERCHANDISE." My voice rose with each word, my fatigue showing. But who wouldn't be angry about someone who'd been like your right arm, through thick and thin, stealing from you? And not just penny-ante either. Major theft. Okay, maybe short of grand larceny, but getting close.

"Are you recording this call?"

"I am."

"I didn't consent to it."

"Ah, I checked. You don't have to. Let's see, I have it written down somewhere ... Here it is: North Carolina's wiretapping law N.C. Gen. Stat. §15A-287 is a 'one-party consent' law. That means only one of us has to consent, and I sure do. And it's legal for me to have cameras in my store. So if you don't want to be recorded, Mary Lou, I suggest you hang up."

And she did.

Fine by me. I was too tired to effectively deal with all this right now. I was still getting over the shock of Abit being kidnapped and my flying more than eight-thousand miles in just four days. But at least I'd let Mary Lou know I was onto her.

I hung up and went back to the videos. As I'd told Mary Lou on the phone, I saw her packing away the goods in a specially made raincoat. She was a great seamstress, so she must have customized it for her shoplifting. It seemed funny that I hadn't noticed the strange cut to the coat when she'd wear it to the store. Or on the videos. But she was my friend, my invaluable assistant manager. I'd just thought she'd put on weight, her turn for middle-age spread. It wasn't until Alex played the recordings in slow motion that I realized what had happened. We'd had a rainy winter and spring, so she'd had a field day in her raincoat.

Early on, Mary Lou had been vital to the success of Coburn's; she'd even run the store almost single-handedly while I was in D.C. for extended stays while Alex recovered from some treatments. That was why I'd given myself a break from the tedium of watching any footage she was in. When I saw her, I fast-forwarded through her scenes because, well, she was one of the last persons I'd ever suspect.

I needed to call her back, or better yet, drive over to Mars Hill and talk face to face. I didn't think she was a flight risk, not with Duane finally landing a good job in construction—at least that's what Myrtle told me earlier when I'd casually brought up Mary Lou, testing the waters with someone who didn't miss much. But Mary Lou had apparently fooled even Myrtle.

Mars Hill was an hour west of here, and I dreaded the drive. I especially didn't want to waste my time going over there if she wasn't home, but I didn't think a phone call would resolve anything. And now that she knew I knew, I'd better act fast.

Annie was fine with closing up, so Rascal and I jumped in the Jeep and headed west. I'd always thought Mars Hill was a strange name—who wouldn't? A few years ago I looked it up on Google. Seems a college over there was named the French Broad Baptist Institute (after the nearby river, not a Gallic tart). In 1859 the North Carolina General Assembly granted it the name Mars Hill College, in honor of the hill in ancient Athens where the Apostle Paul debated Christianity with some of the leading philosophers of the day. If I'd had to choose between the two names, I'd take Mars Hill over French Broad. Or maybe it was a tossup.

I still had Mary Lou's employment records at the store, so it had been easy to find her address. When I pulled up, I was relieved to see her car in the drive—but then apprehension flowed over me like a tsunami. I sat in the car a moment, catching my breath and finding the nerve. I made Rascal stay in the car as I eased out. I kept telling myself I knew Mary Lou, and she wouldn't have done this without a good (at least to her) reason. I was ready to listen.

When she opened the door, she was more composed than I'd expected. "Come on in, Della. I owe you an explanation."

For once, I had the good sense not to say something snarky. I sat in her sparsely furnished living room—just a couch and two recliners. Not even a TV, though plenty of folks in the mountains didn't watch TV for all sorts of reasons—financial, lousy reception, or just denying themselves a little pleasure. That's big around here.

Mary Lou sat down without offering any coffee or tea. After that windy drive—and with one facing me on the return trip—I would have loved a cup of coffee. But when I thought about it, her playing hostess in this situation would have been more than weird.

"I needed the money, so I set up a sort of black market over here," she said, as if that settled everything. And she started to cry, though it seemed like more tissues than tears.

"Of course you did. Just like every other customer of Coburn's. But they don't clean me out. I know. I watched the videos, and I didn't see anyone but you steal anything."

More tears, no words. I didn't want to spend the day in Mars Hill watching her cry, so I tried to hurry her along. "Is it Duane? Is he drinking again?"

"No, no, nothing like that." Sniff. Sniff.

"What about your kids?"

"They're fine."

"Okay, so what gives, Mary Lou? We've been friends a long time, and I'm willing to hear a good explanation."

"I don't have one." Sniff.

"Well, in that case I'm willing to hear *any* explanation."

"I've got a gambling problem."

What? Mary Lou, the most level-headed person I knew? I couldn't imagine her hanging out at tawdry slot machines or blackjack tables or whatever people do in those places. I was speechless.

She went on. "Duane doesn't know about it. He thinks I'm going to visit my mother, but I head to Harrah's over in Cherokee." Sniff. Sniff.

"Where you lose."

"Yes, in a nutshell, that's what happened." More crumpled tissues. Dry ones, from the look of them. "Please help us. I promise I'll pay back every penny. Duane has a new job."

"Oh, for heaven's sake, Mary Lou. I thought you had more sense ..." The look on her face shut me up mid-sentence. She didn't need me to tell her how stupid she'd been. But I wasn't ready to overlook her sticky fingers. "Look, I'm not in the right frame of mind to discuss this now. As the cops say, (I swear Mary Lou flinched at that word), I don't think you're a flight risk. I'll go back to the store and try to come up with how we can fix this. Maybe Duane doesn't need to know. I'll call you in a day or two."

On the trip home from Mars Hill, I came up with a plan. Not that different from the one I'd arranged for another woman a few years ago: make amends and I won't go to Sheriff Horne. I knew Mary Lou needed therapy in the worst way—I can still see how battered her face was that first year I owned Coburn's. Duane had quit drinking years ago, but those earlier transgressions were bound to have left scars. And now this gambling problem. I planned to tell her if she got therapy and made some restitution, I'd keep this to myself.

Rascal and I arrived home after Annie had closed up. I was glad I didn't have to explain myself or make small talk.

Alex thought I was letting Mary Lou off easy, but she hadn't been his friend—or right arm. She'd been a big part of my finally making Coburn's
profitable. Back then.

A COUPLE OF DAYS LATER, I returned to Mars Hill.

Turns out Mary Lou *was* a flight risk.

The house was empty. Neither she nor Duane had strong ties to the area anymore—parents passed, grown kids scattered—so they'd fled. It was bad enough she owed me thousands of dollars, but I wondered what she owed Harrah's. It was a reputable enough outfit, but I still worried about who might come after her.

I hoped they went somewhere safe. Like Montana, where you can get lost under the big sky. Then I remembered Mary Lou hated cold weather. Okay, the Louisiana bayou. I shook my head. What stupid things to be thinking, but I just couldn't make sense of what had happened. And that I was out thousands of dollars. On the other hand, I hadn't missed the money for years, so what had I really lost? Mostly faith in a once-good friend. I took some comfort in the fact that the stealing was over. I could rebuild Coburn's coffers with Annie's good help. And I'd leave the cameras in place.

Chapter 56
Abit

June 26, 2006

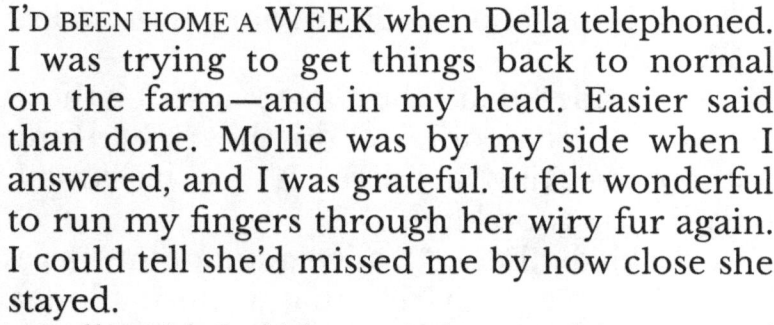

I'D BEEN HOME A WEEK when Della telephoned. I was trying to get things back to normal on the farm—and in my head. Easier said than done. Mollie was by my side when I answered, and I was grateful. It felt wonderful to run my fingers through her wiry fur again. I could tell she'd missed me by how close she stayed.

Della said she'd been tied up at the store and apologized that she hadn't had time to drive out to visit in person, though she would do that later next week. I wasn't sure what that was all about since she didn't come out this way all that much. And to be honest, I was just as glad to not have visitors.

We did all the pleasantries, then she said she wanted to catch me up on the goings-on at the store. I had been wondering about that mysterious mention she'd made in England about trouble at Coburn's.

"Mary Lou has been robbing me blind, Honey," Della said. "I know you and Duane were once best friends, and I didn't want to tell you this before you got settled in again."

That threw me. "Man, I'd never suspect her of doing something like that in a million years. How much did she take?"

"Thousands of dollars' worth."

I whistled real big, and Mollie got excited. I patted her head to let her know we weren't going anywhere. "How'd Duane take it?"

"Well, I tried another one of our white-mails."

"What?"

"I've decided that's the way to describe those times we get people to do the right thing without wrecking their lives. It's like blackmail, only it's the good kind."

I chuckled a little. "You've got a point there. Though don't go sharing that white-mail idea with Conor or Vern. I have a feeling they'd catch on real quick how to use that against me."

"Okay, Honey, I won't." As if I'd been serious. She hurried on. "Anyway, I wanted to give Mary Lou a chance to fix things without Duane ever knowing. But it didn't work out that way."

Della explained how Mary Lou managed to steal so much, sell it on the sly round her home, and then skip town with Duane. I was so taken aback, I didn't know what to say. When there was a long pause on both ends, Della finally said,

"Well, I guess that's all my news ... Oh wait, what is the matter with me? I wanted to tell you that Nigel said Ian had been working undercover for the Met all along. Did you know that?"

"Ian McCafferty?"

"None other. Apparently after he'd given up residency at Her Majesty's prison, he'd cut a deal. Like Nigel, he's a great man to have on the inside, working for the good guys. Marcia is the one who wrote to tell me; apparently she's handling Nigel's emails for him. You know, that's some club they have. I wouldn't mind forming one of those here."

Oncet again I was speechless. Mollie nudged me when I quit petting. Eventually, I heard Della say, "Hey, you still there?"

"I am, but my mind is on fire. You mean that guy I was scared of talking to was working for the coppers? Wished I'd known that at the time. I wouldn't've had to wear my brown trousers of an evening."

She laughed. She knew I was using one of Nigel's favorite expressions. Whenever he was recounting some tight spot he'd gotten into (and when wasn't he?), he'd say that about needing brown trousers.

"Did McCafferty know Clive and Cyril were brothers?" I asked. "I mean, he might've known what Cyril was up to."

"No, he said all that was a surprise. It'd been years since the brothers so much as spoke to one another, even when they crossed paths at the

Dog & Bone. According to what Nigel told me, Clive did try to keep an eye on Baldy, making sure the kid was taken care of. And in his strange way, Cyril seemed to love that boy. At least you said the food was good."

"Hard to give him any kinda credit when you think about all the stuff he made Baldy do," I said.

I got a strong feeling she was holding something back, but then she changed the subject. "Oh, it seems that Ian and Marcia are a number again," her voice going all light and happy.

"Yeah, she'd told me they used to be together, and that basically he was a good guy. He was nice enough to me, but I knew he'd had a bad history. I guess we all need a second chance to do right." I was happy for Marcia, though I hoped Ian *was* the kinda guy she could trust for the long haul. "Did Nigel explain anything more about how things played out? I mean that whole trip was a tangled mess."

"He did. Seems Clive Ownbey had framed Nigella because she'd done him wrong on an earlier job. But I think you already knew that." I had heard some of this before from the horse's mouth (Nigella), but I let Della finish. "That's how the pearls and brooches got into her greenhouse and garden."

"Honestly, Della, if they weren't so scary, I'd say they were just like a bunch of kids. And did Miles ever find out? About, you know, with Nigel?"

"I don't know what you're talking about, and please don't tell me. Nigel did mentioned that Miles had gone off the rails that time you saw him with a gun. He was upset, missing Nigella and feeling threatened by Clive, someone he'd worked with for years."

"Yeah, but the Ownbey gang doesn't seem like the type to look the other way when someone waves a gun in their faces."

"You'll have to ask Nigel for more details. All he said was what I just told you, and that Miles had been doing Ownbey's accounting, so I guess Miles thought he could throw his weight around a little. You know—he knew where all the figures were buried. He was lucky he didn't get swept up with Ownbey's gang members when the coppers came a-calling. How Nigel finds these people I'll never know."

"I reckon the same way flies find stink so fast."

Chapter 57
Della

June 30, 2006

IT WAS WEIGHING ON ME that I hadn't gotten out to Abit's farm. I needed to see for myself how he was doing—and deliver some news that would be hard to hear over the telephone. He hadn't dropped by the store since he'd gotten back, and I'd sensed how low he was feeling when we'd talked on the phone the week before. I hoped I wouldn't make matters worse.

Abit and Mollie came out on the porch when I drove up. Rascal was crying in my ear and scrabbling so hard to get out the window I almost ran over one of Fiona's
garden gnomes. Abit looked as trim as ever. We'd both put on weight in England—hard not to with all the scones and beer and shepherd's pies laden with mashed potatoes. I could tell he'd already taken off his extra pounds; I was still working on mine.

He brought out some lemonade, and we sat on the porch swing together. He'd put it up last summer for the boys, but they were so busy with school and camp and friends, I think Abit used it more than they did.

"So how's the woodworking business? Nose to the table saw?" I asked.

"Getting there."

"And the kids?" I looked around the yard and asked, "Hey, where are they? School hasn't started yet has it?"

"No, they're off with a neighbor friend to Mystery Hill. Remember when Alex took me there?"

"I do. What would that be ... more than twenty years ago? I'll never forget how much you loved that."

"Oh, man. That was such an amazing time for me. Something stirred inside me that day, seeing all those people looking at the unexplainable. Not that different from the way I felt about myself at the time. But that was when I started breaking away from all the darkness I grew up with."

He was quiet for a long moment, lost in thought. When I started to speak, he did too. "I'm sorry, you go first," I said.

"No, I'll wait. I've got a coupla things I want to ask you about."

"Okay, I just wondered how the kids enjoyed their trip to Ireland."

"They had a grand time meeting relatives and seeing new sights. And we all loved seeing Clifden, where Fiona grew up." Another long pause. "But they know something ain't right." I could feel my eyebrow go up. He hesitated before adding, "Fiona's in a bad way. I know some of it's still jetlag. She had to go back to work at the hospital right away, in part because we stayed longer than we'd planned. You know, because of me. But she's also missing her family real bad."

I knew there was more to come, so I waited. "My birthday went uncelebrated, and you know how I feel about birthdays. Conor and Vern did give me stickers for my mando case—one of the Irish flag and the other the coat of arms of Dublin. But nothing from Fiona. And she won't let up about me ruining her trip home. It's like one of Mama's soap operas—everything feels all outta proportion. I just don't see how I ruined *her* trip. But I've apologized and apologized. She keeps on about Johnny Ray Meeks and all his antics last summer and how she couldn't imagine why I still liked Nigel. But she has lots of family to fall back on, even if they're almost four thousand mile away. I don't. What I agreed to do for Nigel didn't seem dangerous; I'd never have done that to her or the boys."

He sipped some lemonade, his throat dry from so much talk. "Besides, Cyril wasn't even part of Nigel's thing. He was his own crook. That's one of the things I wanted to talk to you about. I can't let go of the idea that if it weren't for me bragging and carrying on like I was a big grocery store owner, none of that woulda happened."

"Hey, you were just having a little fun in a difficult situation. You weren't lying to get something; you were undercover, making your legend up as you went. And didn't you say Nigel suggested you play around a little to help you relax?"

"Yeah, but I can't blame him. I did it. Anyways, I'm in the doghouse."

"I bet Mollie likes that." He attempted a smile, an effort falling so short I knew it was too soon for even a hint of humor. "I'm sorry, Honey. That doesn't sound fair of Fiona. But it does sound like something time will heal. She just needs a few more night's sleep listening to the crickets and the creek."

"I reckon. But she's right. What if I hadn't lied?"

"What if, what if, what if. What if you hadn't gone to The Hicks? What if you'd never gone looking for those con artists—and never met Fiona along the way? What if you'd turned right instead of left?"

"Still, I caused this."

"You didn't."

"Did." We both smiled. "We sound like how me and Baldy got."

And there we were, back to Baldy. Abit had told me earlier how he'd thought of not pressing charges, doing one of our white-mails with all kinds of conditions for Cyril to abide by. But the thought of Baldy living under the same roof with Cyril changed his mind. Not to mention the British police would never have allowed that.

"I can still hear his snuffles, Della. And his pleas not to go into care. I keep hoping they'll find his mother, and he can live with her."

"Honey, it didn't go down quite like that."

"Don't tell me Cyril got away."

"No, he's in jail. But there's more." He didn't say anything, so I plunged ahead. "First off, as Baldy told you, his mother ran off, but that was years ago. They can't find her anywhere, and more than likely never will. She hasn't been in their lives for three or four years."

"Oh. He made it sound recent-like. So that means Baldy *will* go into the foster care system. Where is he now?"

"He's in a children's facility." Abit looked so stricken I reached over and squeezed his hand. "He needs special care to deal with all he's been through. I did a little research, and the age of criminal responsibility in England is ten years old—good thing the little bruiser was only nine. He can't be arrested or charged with a crime, so this facility is as far into the legal system as he has to go. He'll get some counseling and other care he needs. And do you remember when Nigel said he had a plan? Well, he knows this couple who want to foster, and apparently they're in a position to pull some strings. With any luck, that's where Baldy will go afterwards. And thanks to Marcia's emails, Nigel is reporting in every week."

He sat quietly for a long moment, letting the rhythm of the swing calm his nerves. "I've never even mentioned Baldy to Fiona. We've got our hands full and money's tight, especially since the trip lasted longer than it was supposed to. She'd just blame me somehow for Baldy going into care."

"Well, maybe someday you'll find the right time to tell her. Don't put it off too long, or she'll be mad about *that*. And Honey, I hate to do this to you, but there's another wrinkle."

He rolled his eyes and sighed. "Could things get any worse?"

"Maybe." He made a motion with his hand for me to go on. "I don't know how to tell you this, Abit, but Baldy was in on the con all along. He and Cyril set it up together. Crime runs in their family, and like Nigel told us earlier, they'd done this to other men. Baldy spilled the beans when the cops brought him in and he got scared."

"I guess if his mother was long gone," Abit said, "all those times he acted like he was hiding from her were fake." I could tell he needed more time to make sense of what I'd just told him. Eventually he asked, "But how did they keep their victims from going to the cops? That doesn't make sense. If I'd needed to, I woulda gone straight to the station when I finally got out."

"Uh, it's a really sordid tale, Abit. Baldy said something about doctored photographs and blackmail. And once Cyril had been paid, they drugged the men and dropped them off somewhere down in Bournemouth, which only added to their confusion about who had done this to them. The cops don't have much hope of ever finding them."

Abit jumped up, his face drained of color. "Well, just for the record, there were *no* photos of me with Baldy. Nothing that coulda even been doctored." He sat back down on the swing.

"I know, Honey. And you're right, there were no photos, so the way I see it, Baldy didn't want to go on with this con. Especially against you."

"So why didn't those other men try to overpower Baldy? They could've. I thought about it."

"Yeah, you *thought* about, but you didn't. And the way Baldy explained it, most of the kidnap schemes took only a day or two—once a family member got the ransom text, they paid up right away. Apparently Cyril chose carefully—men of means who'd rather pay and get it over with. Besides, didn't you say Baldy stayed in that other room? He never got close enough for them to overpower him."

"And if I hadn't bragged about how much money and land I had, this woulda never happened."

We'd been round and round about that; he'd need to work that out on his own. When I didn't say anything, he asked, "So why did Cyril keep me so long?"

I knew that would come up, and as much as it might hurt him, I couldn't let Fiona's flippant attitude go unaddressed. I eased into it softer than she deserved. "It didn't help Fiona was in a different country and thought the texts were scams. That's why it took longer. In fact, it was Baldy that got you out."

Abit would be working on that one later as well. He skipped over it for something easier to handle. "I guess that means Baldy did give me a break, not doing that photograph thing. Even before he unlocked the door and showed me the way out."

"Seems that way." I thought a while about what I wanted to say next. "You know, you gave that boy something he'll live with the rest of his life."

"Oh, yeah, what?"

"You showed him he can overcome a bad upbringing. You turned his head, Abit. He let you go because he knew right from wrong, and you brought that out in him. He's a good boy, and we'll keep tabs on him. Let's make a date—once a month we'll get together and call Nigel and Marcia. She'll know when we're going to call so she can make sure Nigel is around to give us an update."

I felt his shoulders ease. He nodded.

"You said you wanted to talk about two things."

"You've kinda touched on it already. That part about overcoming a bad upbringing. You know how Mama had that club, the Terrapin Preservation Club?

"Yeah, she got me to join the first week I moved here."

"She didn't ever learn to drive, but she sure bossed anyone who did drive her into stopping whenever a terrapin was in the road. You'd have to pull over, and she'd jump out and pick it up by its carapace and move it to the side of the road so it wouldn't get squashed."

"I still do it. It's one of my favorite memories of Mildred."

"Well, I've come to understand this trip was like that for me. It was as though someone reached down and took a heavy carapace offa my back, lifting me up from my past and setting me down somewhere safe. And I'll tell you, it feels good. It's like I know now that people will always do stupid things, politicians will keep throwing their weight round, crops won't grow, rain won't come, and yet somehow good can still come from it. Last summer was frightening, and now Conor has a brother. This year I came through something awful, but I feel lighter."

"Maybe that will help you forgive yourself for talking big about the grocery stores." He just shrugged.

It was getting late, and as much as I hated to leave, I needed to get home. I reached into my purse and pulled out an envelope. "I have something here from Nigel. Something he wanted you to have. A check for $1,000 to pay for your trip to England."

He put his hands up, as though he were warding off evil. "I don't want anything to do with that. I may still consider Nigel a member of our family, but I know too much about the ways he makes his money."

"Okay, give it to Conor and Vern."

"I don't want them spending tainted money."

"Well, what about Baldy? Send it to him."

"How? Where?"

"We'll figure that out."

I left the envelope on the swing when I stood and called Rascal. He and Mollie had played so hard they were both lying by the water bowl, panting. Abit and Mollie walked us to the Jeep. As I drove down his long driveway, I could see him in the rearview mirror, waving.

Chapter 58
Della

July 5, 2006

A FEW NIGHTS LATER, my phone rang. I picked up on the first ring.

"I thought about what you said."

Abit. "Okay."

"And listen, I'm sorry about calling so late."

"Alex just got home, so you're fine."

"Well, I talked with Fiona. I told her all about Baldy, and she shared how badly shaken she'd been. We found some common ground, Della."

"That's great, Honey." I waited for more.

"Back in England I said something to Nigel that confused him. To be honest, it confused me. I told him I was drifting in place. That reality was overrated. Those words just came out from, well, I don't know where. When Nigel said that made no sense, I told him it did to me, but really I needed time to think about it. And believe me, I had nothing but time after that. What I came to see was that the best way for me to live is to have my feet firmly on the ground, but let life flow all round me. You know, drift in place. Nigel, he's dug so deep, I don't reckon he can ever change. And Mama with her strong beliefs? She was rigid as a flagpole, everything had to be the way *she* saw it. But life's not like that. Not a life with family and friends and passersby all following different paths. Not a life lived well."

This was the most Abit had shared with me since he'd gotten home. And he wasn't finished.

"I've surrendered the rest of it. Ever since that carapace was lifted, that's easier to do. Everything was so tangled up, I was just too deep in the forest to see my way clear. Now I know people in the club were actually pretty nice to me. Roy Arthur let me play his mando, Marcia took me to Stonehenge, and Nigel looked after me, in his own way. And little Baldy? He helped me escape. That's really all that matters. I mean, who hasn't gotten mixed up in things that stretched their sense of right and wrong? Like my grocery store lie. Nothing is black and white; it all depends on what's going on at the time. The way I see it, it's not so much what we get ourselves into as how we get out. What matters is how we leave things with one another."

Other than Abit and little Baldy, I hadn't been feeling very charitable toward anyone in that dreadful escapade. That included Nigel and Fiona with her high and mighty ways. I'd worried they'd all taken something from Abit that might never return, and that had scared me. But now I sensed he was on his way back. The fact that he could already think kindly toward people who'd used him in one way or another confirmed it. If I'd been in his shoes, I knew I'd still be furious with each and every one of them.

But then that wouldn't be the first time Abit reminded me to be a better person.

Read an excerpt from the next book in the series, *Up the Creek*, following the Book Club Guide.

YOUR FREE BOOK IS WAITING FOR YOU

Free prequel novelette!

Spend more time with Abit & Della

Learn how Della & Abit met

Takes place 1981-1984

VISIT
https://BookHip.com/CGPGFA

FOR YOUR FREE COPY

OR CLICK <u>HERE</u> TO GET YOUR FREE COPY

ENJOY SIX APPALACHIAN MOUNTAIN
MYSTERIES
FOR ONLY $9.99
*

CHOOSE YOUR FAVORITE RETAILER
HERE.

Dear Readers ...

I hope you enjoyed this book in my Appalachian Mountain Mysteries series. I sure enjoy writing them! I've been a professional writer for several decades now (I got my start in the mountains of N.C.), and it still thrills me when readers write to me. Sometimes they have questions about the stories and the characters. Other times they leave reviews and, well, make my day!

> "Reminds me of *To Kill a Mockingbird* ... finding your books is like finding a rare jewel." ~J.M. Grayson

> "After reading the first book, I read all the others as quickly as possible!" ~ Ruth H.

I'd really appreciate it if you'd take a minute to leave a review. (It's easy—just a sentence or two is enough.) Reader reviews are the lifeblood of any author's career. In today's online world, they can make a huge difference—so thanks in advance.

These days, I spend my time writing my Appalachian Mountain Mysteries series. I started them as a way to share amazing stories from my back-to-the-land experience in the N.C. mountains. I made mistakes by the wheelbarrow load, but I wouldn't take anything for those years.

I get a kick out of hearing from readers, so don't be a stranger! I'd love to hear your thoughts about Abit Bradshaw, Della Kincaid, and the whole Laurel Falls gang. Write me at lyndabooks@pm.me .

Happy reading!
Lynda McDaniel

P.S. I thought you might enjoy an excerpt from the next book in the series after the Book Club Discussion Guide.

P.P.S. And I hope you'll take advantage of my offer for a free subscription to **Spellbound Mystery Magazine**. Weekly issues are packed with fun facts and book recommendations that make finding a good book easy! Learn more at https://spellboundmysterywriters.substack.com/

Book Club Discussion Guide

Deep in the Forest

1. HOW DOES THE book title relate to the story? How many people and situations were "deep in the forest," figuratively and literally?

2. What concepts did the author present in the book involving human interactions and relationships?

3. The British Isles is a departure for the series. How did the setting impact the story? How are Appalachia and Ireland/England similar?

4. Have you ever felt helpless to assist a child who was in peril? What did you do? What couldn't you do?

5. Have you traveled internationally? How were you treated by the host country? Did you encounter prejudices? Discover some of your own?

6. What are the major conflicts in the story?

7. What feelings did this book evoke for you?

8. Have you ever felt your life was not under your control? Who was holding you hostage? How have you held your own life hostage? How did you get control back?

9. How do characters change, grow, or evolve throughout the course of the story? What events trigger these changes?

10. At the end of the book, Abit Bradshaw says:

The way I see it, it's not so much what we get ourselves into as how we get out. What matters is how we leave things with one another.

How do you relate to that notion? How can our mistakes make us stronger? How does this idea give us permission to be human—warts and all?

Excerpt Book 6

Up the Creek

Laurel Falls, N.C.
Summer, 2009
Chapter 1: Abit

Alder trees know no shame. They sprout and grow and crowd out everything that gets in their way. Greedy for life. Like some people I've known.

Those trees were what brought me down to the creek that summer's day. I was sweating from all the sawing and swearing at the pretty little trees just because there were too many of them. I'd worked all morning, carving my way down a good piece of the creek.

By the time I'd stopped for a break, the sun had burned through the morning mist, though wispy patches still hovered, casting a ghostly glow. That was when I saw him. A man, lying crumpled in a place the trees had yet to claim. Half on the bank, half in the creek, his face dangerously close to the water. No sign he was breathing.

I hurried over and pulled him from the water and mud. When I stood again, my head swam, not from exertion but an overwhelming sense of sorrow. And the promise of more yet to come.

I sat a moment, the wet earth quickly soaking into my overalls. I studied the man as he lay there, silent-like. I'd been part of enough police matters to know I shouldn't move him any farther, but that creek was doing its best to suck the life right outta him. Something tugged at me to get him away from there—somewhere dry and warm. And safe.

He wasn't a big man, maybe five foot nine or ten, but dead weight felt twicet as heavy as regular. I ran to the house—up a slow rise and across a couple of acres—and got my wheelbarrow. I would've driven the truck, but it can't get down that far. (Well, it *can* get down that far; it just can't get back up). Besides, I'd never've been able to lift the man into its bed without doing him even more harm.

I bumped my way back down with the wheelbarrow, and as I approached the creek, I stopped short. He'd moved. Just a little, his arm now resting over his head. I let out a breath I hadn't realized I'd been holding.

"Listen, mister, this might hurt some, but do not be afraid." I soothed, as much for me as him. "I don't know where or why you were hurt, but

I am here in good faith." Then I added, "And if you can hear me, I sure would appreciate any help in getting you into this wheelbarrow."

He didn't—couldn't—help, but somehow, by tipping the lip of the barrow down to the ground, I was able to ease him into its bed. He called out some gibberish, likely painful protests, when I tucked his legs into what they call the fetal position.

I pushed that wheelbarrow partway, then pulled it the rest of the way back up that slope. I had to stop three times to catch my breath, and each time I checked to make sure he still had his. I drove that cart with all my might and finally stopped in front of our chestnut log barn.

Half the barn was now my woodshop, and a few year ago I'd built a guestroom in the other half in what used to be cattle stalls. I wasn't that kind of farmer, so no need to worry about them losing their shelter. I had oncet thought about getting more animals than just chickens, but that promise had long ago faded. A number of friends and drifters had stayed in the guestroom, which was nice enough with the maple bedstead I'd made and a quilted coverlet—Bear Paw, I believe the pattern's called. I'd made a small kitchen and a pretty little table and chairs that sat under the window. I'd always enjoyed taking my meals looking outside, and I'd reckoned my guests would too. The window hosted a wooden flower box I'd built years ago, but now only black, bleak stalks remained, like stragglers at a funeral.

I pulled the coverlet offa the bed. No point in getting mud or worse all over it; the sheets would be easy enough to wash. The front door to the room was plenty wide—I'd used the frame that had guided those wide-hipped steers inside—so the wheelbarrow fit through just fine. Somehow, I picked that poor stranger up and settled him on the bed. I was never so happy to hear a groan.

"You're safe now, mister. I want you to know I am here to help you, not hurt you any further. Rest here for a while, and we'll sort things out later. I just hope and pray you won't be bringing any harm to my home. There's enough trouble going on already without you adding to it."

Though I'd just told him to rest, I knew I had to get those wet clothes offa him. Turned out he was harder to undress than my two boys, back when they were small and fell asleep on the way home from a concert or some other outing. I could tell his clothes were made of fine fabrics, even with all the muck and rank smell. A cut above anything from round here. I was able to pull off his soaking wet shoes, socks, and trousers easy enough, but his shirt was another story. I couldn't imagine what he was doing wearing such a fine, thin one—the kind men wear to offices and church—without a jacket. In these parts, he coulda frozen to death, even in the middle of summer. The shirt had stuck like glue, and as much as I hated to, I had to cut it offa him. I just couldn't budge him enough to do any different. I threw the tattered thing in a corner and pulled the sheet over him before rushing next door to my woodshop for a heater. After I plugged it in, I ran to the house for clothes.

I let the screen door slam as I hurried inside to see what I could find. I rummaged through my closet, but my six-foot-three frame called for clothing too big for him. I'd never had any extra weight, which gave me a leanness that registered as sharp angles and boney edges. As I closed the closet door, I caught a quick glance in the mirror. It surprised me to see how I'd grown even thinner than usual. Maybe that was why people, the few folks I'd been round lately, asked me if I was all right.

I sat on my bed and thought about the man. He was a complete stranger to me; I didn't have a clue what his story might be. My mind went to work on the worst things that could happen, like him getting better and trying to overtake me. I got so into it, I actually started to scare myself. Then my thoughts shifted to wondering if he was someone good—even great—who needed my help. That didn't last long. I was soon back to picturing him a ruthless killer.

I hated thinking thataway, but out here in the mountains, away from even the small town of Laurel Falls, I had to consider all the possibilities. And yet didn't that include good things happening too? I wondered what in my makeup kept me from seeing him getting well and offering me treasure instead of slitting my throat. Of course, I knew why. Good things like that didn't happen.

But for now, he was at death's door, and my only concern was keeping him from crossing over. Life is a fragile thing; it can change faster than the weather come March. So the way I saw it, we needed to throw our arms round what we had any given day. And what I had today was a stranger in my guest room, struggling to live.

Long ago, almost twenty year now, I'd made my own religion with kindness at its center. Kindness is mentioned more in the Bible than all the sins and misgivings Mama used to bring up on a daily basis. I'd come to understand the call to kindness when I was on a trip to Mt. Rogers park up in Virginia. I believe Jesus was there that day when wild ponies showed me about living life as each of us are meant to, natural-like. Not Mama's idea of what that life should be for me, certainly not Daddy's. Mine. That revelation gave me such a sense of peace and good will that kindness became my watchword. Lately, the way I'd been living here on the farm, I hadn't given myself much chance to show kindness, and it felt good to feel its warmth again.

Over the years I'd tried—and failed more times than I cared to remember—to show more kindness than the day before. But when you think about it, that's not such an easy task, especially when you take the time to explore the depths of kindness. Oh sure, it's easy to be kind when you're baking a birthday cake for your boy or helping a friend like Della Kincaid move heavy boxes at Coburn's General Store. Or coming to the aid of that stranger, so vulnerable at the moment. But what about harder acts of kindness, like calling an ambulance for him? I'd ignored that idea when it came to mind earlier, not wanting town folk roaming round my place. So who was I being kind to? Likely me more than him. And thinking ahead, was it kind to my boys to have a stranger living amongst us, someone who, for all I knew, could do us harm? My head ached with possibilities. By the time I'd finished arguing with myself, the sun had left that side of the house and the room began to feel cold.

I made myself get up and move to my boys' room. Not long ago I'd bought a few things on sale they'd need to grow into. At 12 year old, Vern was already taller and wider than Conor, even though he was a year younger. I figured his things would have to do. I also grabbed an old quilt we kept in the linen closet.

Back in the guestroom, I could tell the man hadn't moved. He did grumble as I gently placed the quilt over him. I saw a terrible mess on the pillowcase from a seeping wound I'd missed because of his tangled hair and all that creek water, washing it clear at the time. I kept a first aid kit in my woodshop (I needed it more often than I cared to admit); I brought that over and dressed his wound best I could, both for his sake and so I didn't have to look at its gore. I was able to stuff him into the sweatsuit and thick socks and then wrap him in the quilt, tighter than a newborn coming home from the hospital.

Throughout the rest of the day, I kept watch. Sometimes I'd tiptoe in and stand next to his bed, making sure he was breathing. Other times I'd stand by the door, just listening, not wanting to disturb him.

I couldn't help but smile, recalling the time I had the flu real bad, and the boys, back when they were just 8 and 9 year old, would come creeping into the bedroom to make sure their daddy wasn't dead. The first coupla times they did that, I was sick enough I couldn't say anything to assure them that, in time, I would be okay. But as I got better, I had to work hard at not laughing at their little faces, creased with concern, peering down at me. Finally I couldn't hold back, and I started to laugh. They jumped on the bed, and we rolled round together, happy I was back with them. I cherished that memory, especially now.

He came to a coupla hours later.

Up the Creek **and all books in the Appalachian Mountain Mysteries series are available on Amazon.**

Lynda McDaniel Books

FICTION
Waiting for You
A Life for a Life(permafree)
The Roads to Damascus
Welcome the Little Children
Murder Ballad Blues
Deep in the Forest
Up the Creek
Unwrapped
After Dusk
Deep South Trouble
Appalachian Mountain Mysteries Box Set
A Life for a Life Audiobook

NONFICTION
Words at Work (permafree)
How Not to Sound Stupid When You Write
How to Write Stories that Sell
Write Faster Series Box Set